Brilliant Hues

Other Books in the Growing Faithgirlz!™ Library

Bibles

The Faithgirlz! Bible

NIV Faithgirlz! Backpack Bible

Faithgirlz! Bible Studies

Secret Power of Love

Secret Power of Joy

Secret Power of Goodness

Secret Power of Grace

Fiction

From Sadie's Sketchbook

Shades of Truth (Book One)

Flickering Hope (Book Two)

Waves of Light (Book Three)

Brilliant Hues (Book Four)

Sophie's World Series

Sophie's World

Sophie's Secret

Sophie Under Pressure

Sophie Steps Up

Sophie's First Dance

Sophie's Stormy Summer

Sophie's Friendship Fiasco

Sophie and the New Girl

Sophie Flakes Out

Sophie Loves Jimmy

Sophie's Drama

Sophie Gets Real

The Girls of Harbor View

Girl Power (Book One)

Take Charge (Book Two)

Raising Faith (Book Three)

Secret Admirer (Book Four)

The Lucy Series

Lucy Doesn't Wear Pink (Book One)

Lucy Out of Bounds (Book Two)

Lucy's Perfect Summer (Book Three)

Lucy Finds Her Way (Book Four)

Boarding School Mysteries

Vanished (Book One)

Betrayed (Book Two)

Burned (Book Three)

Poisoned (Book Four)

Nonfiction

My Faithgirlz Journal

Faithgirlz Handbook

Food, Faith & Fun:
A Faithgirlz Cookbook

No Boys Allowed

What's A Girl To Do?

Girlz Rock

Chick Chat

Real Girls of the Bible

Whatever

My Beautiful Daughter

The Skin You're In

Body Talk

Everybody Tells Me to Be Myself,
But I Don't Know Who I Am

Girl Politics

Check out www.faithgirlz.com

From Sadie's Sketchbook

Brilliant Hues

Book Four

Naomi Kinsman

ZONDER**kidz**

ZONDERVAN.com/
AUTHORTRACKER
follow your favorite authors

ZONDERKIDZ

Brilliant Hues
Copyright © 2012 by Naomi Kinsman Downing

Illustrations © 2012 by Zonderkidz

This title is also available as a Zondervan ebook.
Visit www.zondervan.com/ebooks

Requests for information should be addressed to:

Zonderkidz, 5300 Patterson Ave SE, Grand Rapids, Michigan 49530

Library of Congress Cataloging-in-Publication Data
Kinsman, Naomi, 1977-
    Brilliant hues / Naomi Kinsman.
       p. cm. — (From Sadie's sketchbook) (Faithgirlz!)
       Summary: When Sadie returns to Menlo Park, California, she finds that she
no longer fits in, especially when one of her father's cases places her in the
spotlight — and in danger — but she turns to her faith, hoping it will see her
through.
       ISBN 978-0-310-72668-5 (softcover)
       1. Interpersonal relations — Fiction. 2. Family life — California 3. Christian
life — Fiction. 4. California — Fiction. I. Title.
PZ7.K62935Bri 2012
[Fic] — dc23   2012018387

All Scripture quotations, unless otherwise indicated, are taken from the Holy Bible,
New International Version®, *NIV*®. Copyright © 1973, 1978, 1984, by Biblica, Inc.™ Used
by permission of Zondervan. All rights reserved worldwide.

Editor: Kim Childress
Cover design: Kris Nelson
Interior design and composition: Greg Johnson/Textbook Perfect

Printed in the United States of America

12 13 14 15 16 /DCI/ 20 19 18 17 16 15 14 13 12 11 10 9 8 7 6 5 4 3 2 1

For my writer friends who challenge
and inspire me and who share my love of
sea wind and crashing waves.

Chapter 1

The Man on the Beach

I kicked off my flip-flops, dropped them on the pile of towels and bags, and chased Pippa across the sand. Salty wind whipped the laughter out of my mouth and carried it out to sea in gusty swirls. All week, my parents and I had unpacked boxes and settled in to our new house, but not until right now, this second, did I feel like I'd really come home. The first days of summer vacation, on my favorite Santa Cruz beach with Pippa. Higgins and Cocoa ran circles around us, barking and nipping at one another's paws. When we splashed into the waves, the icy water drove needles into my bare skin.

"Ow, ow, ow!" I hopped from foot to foot, trying not to let either stay in too long.

"Sadie, look out!" Pips pointed to the crest of white water barreling toward us.

We sprinted toward dry land but the wave slammed into our legs anyway, soaking us to our waists. Pips shrieked and high-footed it out of the water, untangling seaweed from between her toes.

She draped a slimy strand over my shoulder and grinned. "Wanna go again?"

My crazy best friend. No matter how much had changed, Pips was still Pips.

I tossed the seaweed back at her. "Are you kidding me?"

"You're out of practice."

"A year in Michigan can do that to you." I threw her an evil grin. "I'm not sure what *your* excuse is."

Higgins and Cocoa waited, tails wagging, their eyes following my every move.

"Cocoa is gonna tackle you." Pips took the ball out of my sweatshirt pocket and pitched it into the water. Higgins watched, head cocked, as Cocoa leapt into the waves.

I scratched his ears. "You going to learn to swim today, Higgins?"

Higgy licked my nose and then tore into the water after Cocoa.

"Guess that's a yes," Pippa said. "Wanna dry out?"

I brushed the sand off my hands. "Good call."

Higgins and Cocoa caught up to us halfway back to the towels, soaking us again as they shook seawater out of their fur. Pips threw the ball and the dogs chased one another back to the water. Mom and Pippa's mom, Alexis, had found a spot further down the beach where they busily covered their arms and legs with sunscreen. Mom always said that cloudy days gave you the worst sunburns of all. I shivered, but I didn't really mind the cold. Being here at the beach, having Mom with us, was almost too good to be true. It wasn't like her Chronic Fatigue Syndrome was gone or anything. Mom still got tired and had to take it easy lots of the time, but ever since we talked — really talked — and promised each other to stop pretending nothing was wrong, she'd had much more energy.

"I'll get the sunscreen from Mom." The dogs bounded toward us soaking wet from the waves. "You keep the crazies off our towels."

Pips grimaced. "Right. Wish me luck."

Mom and Alexis stopped talking when I got close.

"Secrets?" I asked.

Usually, sudden silences from them ended up with a detour to frozen yogurt or the movies. But as they eyed each other strangely, I wondered if this time wasn't that kind of secret.

"Everything okay?"

Without meaning to, I looked over my shoulder at the rocks on the bluff, where Mom and I used to come to try to catch the wind, back before she got sick. When the wind whipped through my fingers and tugged at the ends of my hair, nearly lifting me up off the rocks, it blew away bad feelings too. Like the time Pips and I got in an enormous fight over which cake to bake for her sister's birthday, or the day my goldfish died. No matter how impossible things seemed when

I climbed up, after trying to catch the wind, I'd climb down light and clean and ready for whatever might come next.

Mom smiled at Alexis. "There Sadie goes, worrying about me again."

"When she's the one plowing full steam into the ocean," Alexis said. "You girls make sure to dry off. It's cold."

I grinned. "No kidding. Can we borrow the sunscreen?"

Mom handed me the bottle. "Sure. And watch Hig, will you? The beach is new for him."

"Did you see his flying leap into the ocean?"

"That's what I mean. He might decide to join the seals or something."

Just then, Higgins slimed me with his sandy nose, and amazingly, dropped the ball. I threw it again and then took the sunscreen back to Pips.

"This game might never end," I told her as we lathered up and the dogs raced toward the ball.

"They'll get tired soon." She pointed to a Labradoodle that bounced over to join Higgy and Cocoa in the waves. "Or distracted."

The three dogs chased one another up the beach, sending foam into the air behind them.

"Doesn't take much to make them happy." I twisted my star earring around in a circle. Before I left Owl Creek for California, Andrew had given me the earrings. They matched the necklace he'd given me for Easter.

"Don't be sad," Pips said. "You're here now, with me. I've been waiting for this all year."

"I'm not sad."

"But you miss Andrew and Ruth and everything." She nudged me, smiling. "I know."

Pips could still see right through me.

She took out her iPhone and jealousy stabbed through me yet again. My parents were making me wait for my 13th birthday—all the way in August—to let me get my own phone.

Pippa tapped her photo app. "While the dogs are busy, I'll catch you up."

The first picture was of all the girls, arms around each other, in front of a bank of lockers.

"This was the first day of school last year." Pips said, turning pages quickly, past pictures of lockers the girls had decorated for friends on birthdays and game days, stopping on a page with the girls all making posters.

"Alice ran for school secretary last year, and lost by three votes to this girl named Margo, so she's been planning next year's campaign ever since."

"Did Bri get contacts?" I pointed to the next picture.

"Yes! And you wouldn't believe how much drama there was for weeks while she figured out how to wear them. I swear, she had to go to the office almost every day because she kept losing them in her eyes."

The next picture showed the girls dressed up in sparkly dresses, with boys standing next to them.

"The Holiday Ball," Pips said.

"Juliet went with Rickey?"

His I'm-about-to-make-trouble grin, and out of control hair clashed with his suit and tie.

"Yeah, and probably you don't want to bring it up, either," Pips said. "He put a lizard in her purse when she wasn't looking."

I could just see Juliet batting the lizard away, dancing like a crazy marionette even after the lizard was long gone.

Pips grinned. "She still hasn't forgiven him."

"I bet."

Pips swiped past picture after picture. Alice organizing pranks around campus, Bri winning an award for a pair of shoes she designed at Spring Break camp, Pippa and Alice holding the 1st place soccer trophy above their heads, grinning wildly. Alice was in a lot of pictures with Pips, and Juliet and Bri were together a lot too. Like they'd paired off, kind of. I played with a loose thread on my jeans and swallowed back worry. I loved all the girls, and I knew they'd be happy I was home now. Still, it seemed like the space I used to fill wasn't there anymore. Not after they'd had all these experiences without me.

Pips swiped quickly past a video of some girl in the mall, and on to another picture of all four girls.

"Who was that?" I asked.

"No one," Pips said, a little too quickly.

"Pips . . ." I said.

But she wasn't looking at her phone anymore. I followed her gaze down to the ocean.

"Where's Higgins?" she asked.

Cocoa was bouncing around in the waves with the Labradoodle, but Higgins wasn't anywhere nearby. My heart started to pound and I stood, scanning the beach. He couldn't have gone far. But what had I been thinking just letting him run wild? I knew better.

I squinted into the sun, and finally saw him, far down the beach. I broke into a run.

"Wait, Sadie—" Pippa said.

I didn't wait. My mouth was still bitter with dread from those few seconds when I thought I'd lost Higgins, and I wouldn't feel right until I had his leash clipped to his collar. As I neared, I realized he was circling a man. Even though Higgins wagged his tail, I slowed. Something didn't feel right about the man. He clearly had treats or something in his pocket that Higgins wanted. The man locked eyes with me, grabbed Higgins' collar and waited. He didn't smile. I stopped a few feet away from the man, not sure what to do.

"Your dog, right?" the man asked. "Sadie Douglas?" Okay, something definitely wasn't right. I wanted Higgins, now. I took a step backward.

"Are you Sadie Douglas?" the man repeated, as though I might not have heard him the first time.

I glanced over my shoulder. Pips had followed me, thank goodness, but she was still far enough away that she probably couldn't hear this conversation. *Hurry, Pips.*

I held out my hand. "Here, Hig."

"It's okay," the man said. "I know your dad. I work with your dad, actually."

"Higgins?" My voice quavered.

"What's going on?" Pippa asked, coming up next to me. "Hello," she said to the man and frowned. "Thanks for catching Higgins for us."

She stepped forward to take Higgins' collar, but the man grabbed her wrist. I bit my lip to keep from screaming. It was like watching one of those movies they show in school about what not to do around strangers.

Sharp barking sounded from behind me, and Cocoa bounded up, his hackles raised. Higgins started barking too and snapped at the man, who let go of both Pips and Higgins, surprised. Both dogs turned toward him, growling. I'd never seen either of them act this way.

"Call off your dogs," the man said.

"Yeah, right," Pips said.

Shoulder to shoulder, Higgins and Cocoa closed in on the man. He backed away, his hands raised. I wanted to grab Higgy and run with Pips up the beach, but then I'd have to turn my back on this man.

"Just tell your dad," the man said. "Tell him that Karl wants to talk to him."

He tossed a piece of paper toward us. "And give him that."

Higgins and Cocoa didn't budge as he turned and jogged away. As the distance between us grew, my muscles relaxed until I collapsed onto my knees in the sand and buried my face in Higgins' fur.

"Um ... What just happened?" Pips knelt down next

to me. "You okay? Who was that guy, anyway? I thought your dad was working with Tyler, from my grandma's church."

I couldn't stop shivering.

Pippa picked up the note and read it. "It says: Be careful who you side with."

She rubbed her wrist and stared after the man. I watched her anger fade away, and the realization of all the things that could have happened come over her.

"Sadie . . . " she said, her voice a little shaky now.

"I know . . . " I whispered.

Mom and Alexis weren't even looking at us. We leashed up the dogs, ran back up the beach, and told our moms what had happened.

Mom grabbed the note from me. "Where's this man?"

Alexis gave Mom a don't-overreact look. "It's okay, Cindy. The girls are okay."

Even though I'd been really scared, Mom's reaction surprised me, almost as though she had expected something bad to happen today. Her hands shook as she stuffed things into her bag.

"Are we leaving?" I asked.

"Girls, grab your things and get in the car now."

Mom rarely used this tone of voice. Pips and I ran for our towels, scooped everything into our arms and raced the dogs to the parking lot. Once we were all in the car, Alexis locked the doors and started the engine.

"What's going on?" Pips asked.

Alexis put the car in gear. "I don't want you girls to worry."

I shot a questioning look at Pips and she shrugged back. Our moms were silent, and in the mirror I could see their matching grave expressions. Something was going on, something bigger than what Pippa and I had told them, something bad enough to swallow up all the air in the car. Higgins curled up in my lap and Cocoa flopped onto Pips. I scratched Higgy's ears, my questions hot and scratchy in my throat, as we turned onto the highway and headed toward home.

Chapter 2

Doorways

Vanilla scented bubbles spilled over the top of the bathtub. I had to turn off the jets and mop up the mess before I could sink back down into the suds and soak away the sand, salt, and fear from the afternoon. My parents' voices rose and fell, the sound traveling up from the kitchen through the vent. Even though I couldn't hear their actual words, I knew they must still be talking about the man on the beach.

I closed my eyes and lay back against the tub. At the beach I'd been afraid, but now, more than anything, I was irritated. Dad had promised that when we moved back to the Bay Area, when he went back to his old job, his cases would be like they used to be. Simple. Boring, even. This first one was something about a test for cancer. Nothing like his work all last year in Owl Creek with the hunters and the bears, where the argument had spilled over into our lives and made everything crazy. Maybe it was selfish of me, but I'd been looking forward to a break from worrying about Dad's work. Couldn't he just be Dad? Dad who obsessed over making perfect eggs, and who could make anyone laugh no matter how bad they felt.

In fact, I *needed* a break. I had enough problems of my own: Andrew, missing everyone in Michigan, trying to fit back in here. I swirled my finger in the bubbles, shaping them into peaks and valleys. Jangly. That's how I felt, like someone had shaken up my insides and now all the parts of me ricocheted off one another, trying to find where they belonged. It didn't make sense, really. I was home now, after being away for so long. Home, where I was supposed to fit perfectly. Settling into Owl Creek had been like inventing a new life—harder than I expected, but at least I had seemed to be moving forward. Now, coming home, felt like going backwards, back to who I'd been before I left. And I was just ... different.

I missed Ruth. And Vivian. And even Frankie, who'd I'd already been away from for a few months, ever since she moved to New York to live with her mom. Then there was the terrible pang every time I thought about Andrew, like iron fists clamping around my lungs.

Maybe tomorrow, when the girls came for the sleepover, I'd start to settle in. I'd figure out how Old Sadie fit, and where New Sadie fit, and stop feeling like I'd developed multiple personality disorder.

My skin was starting to wrinkle. I opened the drain and

turned on the shower, splashing the sides of the tub to get rid of the extra bubbles. Once the soap was gone, I wrapped myself in an oversized towel and went to find pj's.

Probably it would be time to eat soon. Still, I'd wait for my parents to call me, since they obviously didn't want to include me in their conversation. I hadn't had a real drawing session since I'd been in my new bedroom and I couldn't wait to draw every nook and cranny, every angle and shadow. Higgins opened one eye and then closed it again as I sat with him on the bed.

"The ocean took it out of you, huh, Hig?" I scratched his ears and then opened my sketchbook.

Frankie's envelope fell out. It had been waiting in the mailbox when we drove in from our trip across the country. I pulled out the letter, which I'd already read about a hundred times.

Hey Sadie—

Just when I'm about to come back to town, you leave. You're not forgiven. LOL. Dad's spending the summer in Owl Creek, so I get to live with him until September. Yes! Art lessons with Vivian! But it won't be the same without you. We found this project, for all of us—you, me and Viv. We bought a sketchbook from a group of artists. It has a theme—doorways. We're supposed to fill up the sketchbook and then send it in to be part of a national touring art display. Viv thinks we should draw on paper and paste our work onto the pages, collage style. That way all three of us can work on the sketchbook together. And the great thing about that is you can paint or whatever. What do you think? Will you do it with us? I hope so!!! Mail your stuff to Viv's house, well, trailer. I wonder how long she'll have to live in the trailer while they finish rebuilding her house? Anyway, I guess being in the trailer is better than the apartment in Hiawatha. I'll scan the pictures Vivian and I draw too, and send you attachments by email so you can see everything.

Miss you!!

Frankie

I missed Owl Creek. Eventually, I'd find doorways and paint them, but right now, I grabbed a pencil, wanting to draw without planning first. As the image took shape on my page, I realized I wasn't even drawing my room, like I'd thought I wanted to. The curving lines of Pippa's face stared up at me, freckles scattered across her nose, her mouth tipped up in a grin. Her long brown hair was already streaked with summer blonde, probably from her late-season soccer games. When I'd left last summer, we'd been pretty well matched as far as sports went. She was more of a natural athlete than I was, but we'd been able to play together. Now, after all of her practice, we'd for sure be on different teams.

So what was I worried about? That things would be different with Pips now? Was it all the pictures of Alice and

Pippa together? Did I really feel like I wouldn't fit anymore with the girls who'd been my friends forever?

Someone started pounding on the front door. The sound carried clearly up the stairs to my loft — not a please-let-me-in knock. Very definitely, this was an I'm-coming-in-whether-you-like-it-or-not knock. Higgins barked and charged down to the door. I stopped, pencil in mid-air, my insides turning to ice.

"To your mat, Higgins!" Dad's commanding voice echoed in the downstairs hall.

Dad was the only person Higgins obeyed, and only when he used this now-or-else tone of voice.

The knocking stopped suddenly, and Dad's voice, smooth, calming, began, "I'm sorry, you'll have to — "

A voice, gritty with emotion, cut him off. "Just give me a chance to explain."

Something about the man's words drew me, maybe because his voice was vaguely familiar, or maybe just because he sounded so desperate to speak. He sounded the way I felt sometimes, when my feelings seemed ready to explode out of me if I didn't tell someone. I closed my sketchbook, tiptoed over to the landing, and peeked over.

Dad had only opened the door about a foot, and he stood in the gap barring the way into our house. I could hardly see the man, only the side of his face reddened with anger, and his tousled, black hair. The man from the beach. I shivered and rubbed at the goosebumps that now covered my arms.

"I will hear you out," Dad said. "But in my office, where

we can record your statement and try to get to the bottom of—"

The man cursed and then shouted, "I don't care about protocol."

Dad didn't raise his voice. "Coming to my house, talking to me outside working hours, can only damage the mediation process."

The man slammed his fist against the doorframe. "Listen to me."

Dad began to turn his head toward the landing, as though he sensed me watching. I ducked down behind the ledge just in time, and heard him walk outside and close the door.

I didn't dare go downstairs, but I had to hear more, or at least know that Dad was okay, out there with the crazy man.

Carefully, quietly, I slid my front window open until I could hear their voices again.

"...Unreasonable," the man was saying.

"That's what mediation is all about, Karl," Dad said. "Figuring out what is reasonable and deciding on a logical course of action."

Now I had a name at least—Karl.

"There is no logic with Tyler," Karl said. "He's been like this since we were kids. Always wanting to save the world, as though he can invent some magical device and no one will ever be in pain again."

"But you knew this about him when you started the project," Dad said.

"I didn't know he'd be so stubborn and blind," Karl said. "I didn't know he'd want to wait to test people until it was too late."

"Tests haven't been conclusive either way," Dad said. "We don't know that Tyler's plan won't work."

"Testing kids." Karl spat out the word kids as though it tasted as bitter as ash. "Are *you* going to explain to a dad or mom or brother that you're sorry, but the treatment just didn't work? You're sorry they hoped so hard and went through so much, but due to circumstances— " his voice cracked and for an astonished minute I thought he might be crying. Crying?

"Karl ..." Dad began.

"I will get what I want." Now Karl's voice was low and threatening. "No matter what. Having me on your doorstep will be the least of your problems."

"Karl, you cannot continue to harass my family. We have to— "

"What? Follow protocol? Sure thing, Matthew Douglas. I'll make absolutely sure to dot my i's and cross my t's."

Footsteps sounded on the porch, as though Karl had pushed past Dad. He strode out from under the eaves and I watched him wrench his car door open.

Dad called after him, "Karl ..."

Karl squealed out of the driveway. I felt colder than I had on the beach. The conversation didn't piece together. The crazy guy from the beach, Karl, clearly disagreed with Dad's client, Tyler, about the device. Karl had mentioned testing kids. For cancer? Why would that make Karl so angry?

"I need to report an incident," Dad said, still outside.

He must have called the police.

"Yes," Dad continued. "I'm a mediator and one of the parties dropped by my house and threatened my family. He also approached my daughter and her friend earlier today at the beach. He grabbed my daughter's friend by the wrist."

There was a long pause before Dad continued. "No, he didn't force entry." After another pause, he sighed heavily. "He seemed unstable, but no, he didn't hurt me or anyone else." Dad listened and only barely controlled the irritation in his voice as he said, "Yes, I understand. Still, I'd think you'd want to do something *before* he actually commits a crime."

Dad said goodbye and as the front door opened and shut, I quietly closed the window.

"Sades," Dad called up to me. "Come on down for dinner."

I swallowed hard, strategizing. Dad would know I'd heard part of the conversation, but not that I'd heard it all. Should I pretend I hadn't eavesdropped? Or just let all of my questions tumble out? Would I even have a choice once I looked Dad in the eye? I shoved my hands into my pockets and tried to look relatively normal as I headed downstairs.

From: Sadie Douglas
To: Ruth Manning
Date: Saturday, June 5, 8:21 pm
Subject: Drama

So I meant to write you an email tonight anyway, to catch up
on all the news... but now I have to tell you what's going on.
I thought it was bad in Owl Creek with the hunters. Well, now
there's this crazy guy who's all upset with Dad about the case
he's mediating, and he showed up on our porch. Dad called the
police, but they can't do anything unless the guy commits a
crime. I don't really get what this guy is upset over. Dad didn't
want to talk about it at dinner. He said he'd rather not involve
me. Like I'm not involved. The guy followed us to the beach and
he grabbed Pippa's wrist. She's okay and everything. But still.
Anyway, when I know more, I'll let you know. What's going on
with you? I hear Frankie is back in town. What else is going on?
How are the bears? Are the cubs starting to grow? Have you
seen the spirit bear?

Andrew still hasn't emailed me yet. Do you think I should write
to him? I know we're probably never going to see each other
again, so it's pointless for me to even be worried about this.
But I can't help it. I miss him.

I'll attach some pictures of my new room, because at least
that's a good thing. It reminds me of the Tree House, because
all you see out the windows are branches, and it has all these
odd corners and angles. I wish you could see it. I miss you.

Send me all the news.

From: Sadie Douglas
To: Frankie Paulson
Date: Saturday, June 5, 8:30 pm
Subject: Have you drawn a doorway yet?

If you have, send it to me. I need some ideas. Pippa and I are going to San Francisco in a few days with our moms, so I will probably find my first doorway then. Since Pippa's sister, Andrea, is going away for the summer to an arts camp, I think we'll be able to convince our moms to take us wherever we want to go, at least for a little while.

How's everything else? How's being back with your dad?

Chapter 3

Sleepover

"Sadie, Sadie, Sades!" Pippa pounded up the stairs to my loft, Higgins on her heels.

She dropped her bag on the landing and fought off Higgins as he licked her face.

"Down, Higgy," I pulled him away from her. "You'd think he hadn't seen you for months."

"Well, yesterday was a long time ago." She kissed Higgins on the top of his head. "You weren't kidding. Your new room is like a tree house. And the entire upstairs is yours?"

"I know. Crazy, isn't it?"

She inspected my walk-in closet and the enormous bathroom. "Good thing you're still in our school district, even all the way out here."

"All the way out here? It's only ten minutes from school."

"It feels like another universe. We drove past three horse farms on our way out here."

I wished I could fall into the easy pattern of conversation with her, wanted to be in the mood for a sleepover with the girls, but I couldn't stop thinking about crazy Karl.

"Pips, the guy from the beach came to the house last night."

"What happened?" She sat on my bed, wide-eyed.

"He shouted a lot and said he'd get his way no matter what."

"What did your dad say?"

"That's the thing. Nothing. He wouldn't tell me anything."

Pips rubbed her wrist. "Well, I sure don't want to see that guy again. He's creepy."

She went over to the three paintings on my wall, obviously trying to change the subject. I couldn't blame her. I didn't want to think about Karl either.

"Wow!" Pips said.

I walked over to stand next to her, feeling a little shy. Vivian and I had finished the paintings just before I left Michigan. The first was of me and Higgins curled up in the old Catholic church, our hair tipped with gold as the sunrise glowed through the stained glass windows. The second was Ruth on the beach, her hair and clothes wild in the wind, sunlight streaming down on her through a break in the dark clouds. The last was Ruth, Andrew, me, and Higgins, sitting on the rock near the Tree House, our noses and cheeks bathed in moonlight as we watched the stars.

"I thought your drawings were good, but these . . ." Pips said.

"Paint is my thing, I guess. You like them?" I couldn't resist asking.

Pips gave me a well, duh look. "Yeah. Especially the light. How did you make the paint glow like that?"

"The color only looks like it glows because of the contrast. White and gold look brighter the closer they are to the dark."

"The light means something in all of these paintings, doesn't it?" Pips asked.

Leave it to Pips to ask the uncomfortable question. I squirmed, not sure I wanted to tell her more. It was one thing to email Pips about prayer and all my questions about God, but it felt strange to talk out loud about something so personal.

"I was trying to paint the way it feels when you know God is with you. The way the light and the air feels, charged somehow, with something bigger than you."

Just then the doorbell rang, and Higgins bounded down the stairs. Even before Pippa and I made it all the way to the door, noise spilled into the entryway. Juliet, Alice, and Bri hurried inside, already arguing over who had first dibs on Juliet's brownies. Higgins bee lined for the Tupperware, and nearly bowled Juliet over.

She held the Tupperware over her head, spinning in place to get away from the attack, making the high-pitched shriek that only Juliet could make. "Brownies aren't good for dogs!"

"Higgins, let Juliet be," I called.

Before I could catch his collar, he made one more flying leap.

I yanked him into a sit. "Down, Higgy."

"Whoa, Sades!" Bri dropped her bag and gave me a big hug. "This house is so cool. Like a cross between a ship and a tree house."

Bri headed straight for the wooden steering wheel that the previous owner had installed on one of the thick columns. "Ahoy, ye landlubbers!"

"You guys are so weird." Alice said

"You guys, come check out upstairs," Pips said.

I took Higgins to the kitchen and closed him in. "Mom, can you watch Higgy for a minute while we have brownies?"

"Just don't spoil your dinner. Dad will be home with pizza in about an hour."

"Like pizza's so much healthier than brownies."

Her eyes sparkled as she said, "I could make you all a nice healthy salad instead."

Higgins flopped onto the floor and sighed.

I laughed. "My thoughts exactly, Hig."

Upstairs, the girls were already draped around the room — on the bed, leaning on pillows, their bags in a comfortable pile on one side of the room. A real sleepover just like old times.

"Sadie gets the first brownie." Juliet passed me the Tupperware, swatting Alice's hand away as she tried to steal one en route. "She's had to wait the longest to have one."

Pips sighed. "Yeah, I guess that's only fair."

After I took a brownie, I passed the Tupperware to Pips, starting the free-for-all. After less than a minute, only crumbs were left.

Alice licked off her fingers and then pulled a pile of brochures out of her bag. "Now that Sadie's here, it's time to decide."

"On ...?" I asked.

"Camps!" Juliet said. "I vote for cooking camp."

"You don't need cooking camp," Pips said. "You're already a chef."

"I might need a new specialty," Juliet said. "We can't eat brownies all the time."

Alice passed me one of the brochures. "There's a four week outdoor camp, where you sleep away and go on rope courses and do arts and crafts and hiking and boating and everything."

Juliet grabbed the brochure with the picture of the professional kitchen on front. "Or, there's cooking camp."

Alice ignored her and held up another few brochures. "There's some day camps: horseback riding, or dance, or art ..."

"I was thinking about helping at the Explorer's camp at my Grandma's church this summer, too," Pips said.

Alice frowned. "But we can't all do that together."

"I don't know, I mean we could," Pips said, but shrugged when Alice still didn't smile. "Not if you'd feel uncomfortable, though."

"I can't see my parents being okay with me teaching at a Christian summer camp." Alice kept her voice light, but I knew this was an uncomfortable topic between them. Over email, Pips had told me about Alice's reaction when Pips started going to church with her grandma. Alice's parents were atheists, I knew, and I guess Alice was too. At least she said she didn't believe there was such a thing as God. But Pips never pushed her beliefs on anyone else, so it seemed like Alice was overly touchy about it.

"I don't think it's like that, exactly," Pips said. "I mean, the camp is at church, but no one would be preaching or anything."

Annoyance crept into Alice's voice. "I'm just trying to think of things to do together, that's all. If you guys want to do your own things over the summer, that's fine."

"No, Alice, it's not ..." Pips started.

"No big deal," Alice said, but we could all tell it was by the way she stuffed the brochures back into her bag.

Bri sat up on the bed, breaking the silence. "I've been meaning to ask you all, you know how Margo conned her mom into signing up for the design classes I've been taking in the city?" Something about the way she looked at Pips and then the others made me feel like I was missing something. "Well, she's signing up for design camp too, and I might need your help."

Alice frowned. "I can't go to camp in the city. My parents could never get me there."

"There's cooking camp," Juliet repeated.

Bri ignored Juliet. "I'm serious. I'm already signed up for design camp next week. It's a weeklong design competition, and at the end, the winning team gets to work with a real designer for another week or maybe even more. You know how Margo is. She's decided she has to win."

"Wait, are you saying you want us to—" Juliet asked.

Alice cut her off. "We're getting off topic."

Juliet raised an eyebrow at Alice, and then glanced questioningly at Pippa, who watched me, her expression unreadable.

"What?" I asked as the silence thickened in the room. "Who's Margo?"

"Which camp sounds fun to you, Sadie?" Alice asked, as though she hadn't heard my question.

I turned to Pips. "Wasn't Margo the girl you said ran for school secretary?"

Alice cut Pips off before she could answer. "We'll talk about it later."

I looked from Bri to Juliet to Alice and finally to Pips, the sick feeling growing in my stomach the longer the silence stretched. "Um ... what's going on?"

Pips gave the others an exasperated look. "You guys. We should tell Sadie."

Alice sighed. "Right. We just need to discuss it first, that's all."

"Then stop talking about this," Pips said. "You're making her feel left out."

Perfect. Now they were talking about me as though I

weren't here. My chest started to burn — that I'm going to cry any minute feeling.

Downstairs, the front door opened and closed, and Dad called, "Pizza!"

Everyone jumped up as though a fire alarm had just rung. It wasn't just because of dinner. They wanted to get away from the awkward conversation. Away from me.

I blinked and blinked again. I would not cry.

Pips put her arm around my shoulder before following the others downstairs. "Don't worry, Sades. It's nothing. I promise."

I couldn't help it. Tears filled my eyes and I had to turn from her to brush them away.

"Come on," I finally said, avoiding her eyes. "Let's go eat."

Chapter 4

Secrets

By the time Pips and I pushed through the kitchen door, the other girls were already loading slices onto paper plates. They sat around our wooden kitchen table and dug in.

Mom laughed. "I see the brownies didn't spoil your dinner."

"If we went to cooking camp," Juliet said, "We could make gourmet pizza."

"What's this about camp?" Mom asked.

"We're trying to decide on a camp we can all go to together," Bri said. "And Juliet won't let up on the cooking thing. But I think we're going to design camp first."

"What's design camp?" Mom asked.

"Who's Margo?" I wanted to ask. Instead, I said, "So Dad, are you really going to take us waterskiing soon?"

Hopefully I could steer the conversation away from camp and their secret. Talking about it felt like poking a bruise to see if it still hurt.

"Sure thing, if you all want to go?" Dad grinned his motorboat grin. "No promises on smooth sailing, though."

The other girls started to chatter about their waterskiing records, and even Mom was distracted from her conversation with Bri.

"You've got to promise to be more careful," Mom said to Dad. "Someone will get hurt, the way you whip them around behind the boat like that."

Dad squeezed my shoulders and took a bite of the pizza slice I still hadn't touched. "Better hurry up, Sades, or someone might eat your pizza."

I forced myself to take a bite. "Just waiting 'til the cheese cooled down."

The girls started telling stories on one another. Juliet's lizard story made everyone laugh so hard tears streamed down their cheeks. I tried to join in, but something deep down ached, and my laughter was only half-hearted. My friends had a secret, and even Pips was in on it.

They ate every last slice of pizza and then Juliet leapt to her feet. "Lip sync time!"

The girls raced each other upstairs and dug in their bags for wigs and crazy striped and polka-dotted clothes. Apparently their lip sync for school had a mismatch theme. They did the entire song without cracking a smile. I tried not to feel left out, but I couldn't get past the empty feeling that kept growing inside me. After the song was over, they turned up the music, so we could all dance and sing. I danced too, trying to act like nothing was wrong. Finally, Dad came up and begged us to stop making it sound like elephants were dancing on the roof. Maybe at someone else's house we would have argued, but everyone knew Mom needed her sleep. I had never been so grateful for the dark, as we turned out the lights and climbed into our sleeping bags. No more pretending. Alice and Pippa whispered scary stories until Juliet started to snore.

Alice giggled. "Me too. I'm going to sleep."

After we all said goodnight, I rolled onto my back and stared at the ceiling. Pippa would tell me tomorrow, when the girls went home. She wouldn't leave me out for long. But what secret could be so bad that they had to hide it from me? It was a long time before I fell asleep.

The next morning, none of us woke up until Dad called, "Breakfast, girls!"

The air was sweet with the smell of pancakes and maple syrup. I blinked the sleep out of my eyes. Everyone else looked just as groggy as I felt as we crawled out of our sleeping bags and headed downstairs. I hadn't even thought of checking the clock, but it must have been around three before Alice and Pippa stopped telling stories. Even Higgins took the stairs slow.

Dad dished up plates of pancakes and then took coffee down the hall to Mom.

"So ..." Juliet looked around at all of us as the kitchen

door swung closed behind Dad. "Anyone have plans this week?"

"Sleeping in," Alice said.

"We should at least go to a movie," Bri said. "And design camp is next week."

Camp again. I put my fork down, and pretended not to see Pippa's worried glance.

Pippa cleared her throat "Yeah. Maybe later this week we should get together and talk camps and do something fun."

Alice pushed a piece of pancake around her plate. "We don't have to all do camp together, if you don't want to."

"No one said that, Alice," Juliet said. "Anyway, I think design camp sounds fun. And it's only a week, so we'd still have time to do cooking camp later."

The doorbell rang, launching Higgins into a barking frenzy. I followed him down the hall and answered the front door.

Bri's mom stood smiling on the porch. "Still in pj's, I see."

"We're finishing up breakfast." I held Higgy back so he wouldn't jump up on her. "Do you want some pancakes?"

"The little one is sleeping in the car, so I should probably wait out here. Will you send Juliet, Alice, and Bri out as soon as you can?"

Pippa's mom was driving Andrea to the airport this morning, so Pippa was going to stay over a little longer. Fortunately, because I needed some answers. For a few minutes the girls scurried around, packing up and carrying everything out to the SUV. Pips and I waved them off, all-

40

smiles, but as I closed the front door, the silence made my stomach tangle into knots.

"Sadie . . ." Pips began.

I glanced at my parents' closed door. "Let's talk upstairs."

On the way up, I realized I was once again on the verge of tears. Not sad tears, but angry ones. How could my friends leave me out like this? I leaned against the bookshelf and Pips sat on the bed. Higgins jumped up and put his head in her lap, oblivious to the tension between us.

"Look, Sadie, it's no big deal," Pippa began.

I had so many questions I didn't know what to ask first.

"Alice, Bri, Juliet, and I started this secret club," Pippa said. "You'll be part of it, of course, if you want to be. We swore we wouldn't tell anyone, not anyone, but I never meant you."

A secret club? What were we, in third grade?

"What's the big secret, Pips?"

"I should ask the girls, I guess, before saying anything. But you won't tell anyone." She grabbed a pillow and hugged it tight to her chest. "You know how kids from three elementary schools come to our middle school, right? And some of the new girls started pushing kids around, picking on them, lying about them, that kind of thing."

"Spit it out, Pips."

"None of the teachers do anything about the bullying, not really. Maybe they don't see it, or maybe they're too busy, or who knows. Anyway, this girl, Jaylia—who was jealous because she hardly plays in soccer games and Alice is, well, you know… good—she lied to Alice's homeroom teacher and said Alice cheated on a test."

"Alice wouldn't cheat."

"No. Jaylia planted a handwritten test key in Alice's backpack, so Alice got suspended for three days. She had to sit out of a whole week of soccer practices and the game that weekend."

She might as well have told me they'd gone to the moon and back and hadn't bothered to mention it. "Alice got suspended and no one told me?"

Pippa squished up the pillow even tighter. "Everything happened so fast. At first we didn't know what to do. I thought Alice and I could just cold-shoulder Jaylia in games, you know, never pass her the ball. But Bri said Jaylia wouldn't know why we were treating her that way. I mean she might guess, but it might not be enough to stop her from lying about someone else, or even about Alice again."

Pips tossed the pillow aside and started pacing around the room. Higgins came over to nuzzle my hand. I scratched his ears, waiting for the rest of Pippa's story.

"And then at the mall, in the candy store, we saw Jaylia slip a bag of candy into her pocket. Her back was to us. We followed her out of the store, and Juliet had her cell phone—it does video recordings. Anyway, we forced Jaylia to admit she'd stolen the candy on video. She didn't want us to call the security guard over right then, obviously. So, she did what we asked. And we told her if she ever lied about anyone else, we'd show the video."

I frowned. "Isn't that like blackmail?"

Anger flashed in Pippa's eyes and her voice was hard when she said, "It worked, Sadie. And Jaylia hasn't done anything mean since."

"So that's the secret? That you're blackmailing this girl?"

Pippa glared at me. "Since we managed to stop Jaylia from bullying people, we realized we could do it again, you know, to stop other bullies. Alice, Bri, Juliet, and I swore we'd never tell anyone, that it would be super top secret."

I sighed and sat on the window seat. "So, who's Margo?"

"You know how Juliet is sensitive about her weight. Margo's been teasing her all year, making mean comments the teachers never seem to hear. And Margo edged Bri out of the lead part in the spring play. And I told you she beat Alice by three votes to be school secretary. But all the teachers think Margo's perfect, of course."

"So Margo's your new target?"

Either Pippa didn't hear the sharp tone in my voice or she chose to ignore it.

"Sadie, you have to help us with this." She grabbed my hand, giving me one of her believe-me-or-else looks. "You'll see how great it feels. To stop someone from picking on other people — really stop them. It's amazing."

"But..." I pulled my hand away. "Aren't you just treating them the way they're treating other people?"

She gave me an incredulous look. "Sadie, we're not lying about them."

"No, but ... You can't just do whatever you want as long as it ends up okay, Pips."

43

"We're not just doing whatever we want, Sadie." Pippa had raised her voice, and we both glanced toward the stairs.

Neither of us wanted my parents to hear this conversation. Pips shook her head. "You don't understand."

I didn't want to fight with Pippa. And right now, I wasn't exactly sure why I was so uncomfortable. Maybe, hopefully, because their secret club was all-wrong, but what if I was just angry about being left out?

"Sadie, we're trying to do a good thing. I swear." Pips walked over to my paintings again, her back to me. "It's like what you said about these paintings—how you can feel God with you?"

She turned to look at me, her expression totally sincere. "It's like that. When we're standing up to someone, it feels so right, Sades. I promise. I know it sounds a little . . . "

When her voice trailed off, I realized I must have been giving her a totally disbelieving look. I couldn't help it. She didn't really think God wanted her to gang up on people, did she? I knew I should say something, tell her how wrong I thought this was, but the words stuck in my throat. What if I said something and made her truly angry? Already my friends felt so far away. Pippa might still be Pippa in lots of ways, but she was totally different in others.

"Girls?" Mom's voice called up the stairs. "Pippa's mom is here."

Neither of us said anything as Pippa picked up her bag and went to the stairs.

"See you tomorrow, Sades," she finally said.

"Okay. Yeah," I answered, wishing my voice didn't sound so small and sad.

"Okay," she said and walked slowly down the steps.

I should have followed, should have stood on the porch to wave goodbye. But I just couldn't. Instead, I threw myself on the bed and squeezed my eyes shut. *What do I do?*

From: Sadie Douglas
To: Ruth Manning
Date: Monday, June 7, 2:13 pm
Subject: Re: Kid Disaster

Ruth,

Ha ha! I'm glad you finally caught the frog, and that you didn't have to sleep knowing he was hopping around the house. I'm actually kind of surprised your brother and sister could trap a frog in the first place. At least now they know a bucket with a baking sheet over it isn't enough to keep a frog from breaking loose.

It was nice to laugh... thanks for the funny story. And I'm so so so excited that you're babysitting to save up money to come see me. I can't wait!

Nothing else has happened with the guy from Dad's work, but I can't stop worrying about him. And Pippa and the girls have kept this crazy secret from me all year... they're ganging up on mean girls from school to stop them from being bullies. Doesn't that seem wrong? Treating people the way you don't want them to treat others? Pips and I got in this big fight about it today and when she left, we were barely talking. Tomorrow we're riding the train up to San Francisco with our moms, and after we do some sightseeing, Dad will drive us all home. He works up in The City. I guess I'll just try to act like nothing's wrong when I'm with Pips. I don't want to lose all my friends, Ruth. What do I do?

Oh, and Dad won't stop going on about how he wants us to be careful and watch out for Karl. As though I need something else to worry about.

You really think I should write to Andrew even if he doesn't write me first? I don't know...

Chapter 5

The City

As we walked out of the train station toward the Embarcadero, I remembered why I loved coming to San Francisco. Palm trees lined the waterfront street, and seagulls swooped between skyscrapers. The air smelled of ocean and roasting coffee and possibilities. Pips had seemed almost normal when we all met at the train this morning, and we hadn't talked about the secret club at all on the ride up. For now, I hoped it could stay that way. I didn't like the idea of my friends ganging up on someone, even if that person was a bully. And I couldn't imagine taking part in it. But if I didn't join in, I'd be even more on the outside.

As we crossed the street, Alexis said, "Let's hail a taxi and ride down to the pier, so we don't waste all our energy walking there."

Alexis was right, of course. The pier was about two miles down and if Mom walked there, she'd probably be finished for the day. Even I might want to put my feet up if I walked that whole way. But I didn't feel like getting inside a taxi right now either. I wanted to see the city. Behind us a bike bell rang.

"Need a lift, ladies?"

We turned to see a guy on a four-seater bike-cart.

"You can manage us all?" Mom asked.

"No sweat," the guy said. "If you're headed down to the pier, I'll give you my famous tour, much better than a taxi ride."

We piled in and he drove us three or four blocks before stopping. "The Ferry Building," he said. "Head inside and grab the treat of your choice. I'll wait for you here."

The stalls were stuffed with loaves of sourdough bread and cheese and there were even trays of ice with fresh crabs. We sampled olive oil and ripe berries. In the end, Pips and I decided to share a basket of strawberries. Mom bought artichokes, tomatoes, cheese, and bread to take home for dinner, and Alexis found snap peas, organic olive oil, and balsamic vinegar. I searched for interesting doors, but nothing caught my eye. We carried our treasures back to the cart and surprised our driver with a plate of samples and a fresh baked snicker doodle.

"Off we go to the pier!" He pushed off and wove through the crowds of people.

As we passed a man in a tuxedo jacket outside a restaurant, he shouted, "Get your clam chowder here!"

We all jumped, especially Mom. She glanced back over her shoulder, like she expected the man to suddenly transform into Karl.

"It's okay, Mom," I said.

Our driver—we'd now learned his name was Jack—pointed out Levi's Plaza Park, where there was a museum all about blue jeans and this huge fountain where water spilled over large granite blocks. Kids splashed and played.

It was only a few more blocks to Pier 39, and we could hear the seals barking.

When we reached the main turn around, Jack pulled over and let us off. "Don't forget to have some clam chowder. And of course, don't miss Ghirardelli! I'll be back in three hours in case you want a return ride."

Alexis gave him a big tip, and we headed down to the water. Like usual, Pips and I ran ahead of our moms, all the way out to the furthest point on the dock that we could go. Seals lounged on the rocks, filling the air with their laugh-like barks and fishy smell.

Pips laughed and plugged her nose. "Ick."

I snorted and then regretted it, because now I could even taste the old-fish stink. "I always forget how bad they reek."

"Race you back?" Pips said.

It almost felt like yesterday hadn't existed. "Sure!"

We dodged people on the sidewalk and just as we plowed into Mom and Alexis, a man poked his head out of two bushes that he was holding and growled.

Pips and I screamed and nearly leapt out of our skin.

People all around us laughed, as though they'd been watching, expecting him to scare someone. The guy sat with his back against a trashcan and wore a green coat and hat and face paint. He pulled the bushes back together, and I took a few casual steps away, like he hadn't actually scared me. Mom had gone totally pale.

"Mom, it's okay." I helped her to a bench. "He's that street performer that scares people. We've seen him before. Remember?"

But tension rippled across her shoulders and she held her purse so tightly her knuckles were white.

Alexis shrugged at the still-gathered crowd and gave a forced laugh. "Picked on the wrong people, I guess."

Mom shivered and looked over her shoulder.

"Are you cold, Cindy?" Alexis asked.

"Maybe I should buy a sweatshirt," Mom said, but I got the feeling she wasn't really cold. "And then let's find clam chowder. You girls must be hungry."

We crowded into a tourist shop filled with I Heart SF gear, and Mom found a hooded sweatshirt with the Golden Gate bridge embroidered on the back. Pips and I riffled through keychains and postcards, but in the end, we didn't buy anything. Across the street, we spotted an outdoor food court. Mom and I circled until we found an empty table, and Alexis and Pips joined the clam chowder line.

Smells of cream and garlic and baking bread filled the air. My stomach growled. Mom's glance flitted from face to face as we sat down in the metal chairs.

"Mom, do you really think Karl would follow us or find us out here? Why would he?"

She set purse on her lap and massaged her hands, trying, I know, to relax. "You're right, Sadie. He's just unpredictable. Dad thinks Karl will keep pushing until he gets his way."

"But how will following us around help him?" I asked.

"It's not logical. That's the thing. When people aren't logical, that's when they're truly scary." Mom sighed. "Sorry, Sadie. I didn't mean to say that. I don't want you to worry."

Just then, Pips and Alexis walked over to the table, each balancing two trays in their arms.

"Lunch is served!" Pips set a bread bowl filled with clam chowder in front of me.

I scooped up a spoonful, and blew on it until it was cool enough to sip. The chowder was warm and creamy, and with each bite, I felt a little warmer, even though the wind continued to bite at my cheeks and fingers. Only in San Francisco could it be so cold in the middle of June. As I ate, I scanned the plaza for doors. I still hadn't found one I wanted to draw.

"So ..." Pippa said after a while, when we'd all eaten most of the actual chowder and had started tearing off pieces of the bread bowls. "Have you decided about design camp, Sadie?"

Before I could answer, Mom asked, "What is this camp?"

I'd have to sell this well. "Bri's been taking design classes here in San Francisco, and next week she's competing for an internship with a real designer. She asked us to be her team."

"Can we go, Mom?" Pippa asked.

Alexis and Mom had one of those silent conversations that usually meant no.

"I don't think I want you in the city on your own," Mom finally said. "Isn't there something closer to home you could do?"

"You were talking about being a junior counselor at Explorer's Camp, Pippa." Alexis backed up Mom immediately. "How about that?"

Pippa eyed me uncertainly. "I'm not sure Sadie wants to work with little kids."

"Didn't Jess say she wanted someone to teach art?" Alexis asked. "That's right up Sadie's alley."

Had she and Mom planned this ahead of time?

"I want to go to design camp," I said. "The girls wanted to stick together this summer."

Mom continued as though I hadn't spoken. "I do like the idea of camp at church, Alexis. Teaching art, Sadie? So perfect for you."

I felt like tossing my empty tray across the room. "Isn't anyone listening to me?"

Mom closed her eyes and rubbed her temples, but I wasn't about to back down.

Finally, she sighed. "Sadie, this isn't Owl Creek. I know we allowed you to roam around with your friends there, but here you can't just be unsupervised. Particularly with Karl . . ."

I knew I should stop, but arguments kept tumbling out

of me. "It's not like we'd be on our own at camp. They'd have counselors or teachers or something."

Mom's eyes started to get that hard look that meant I was about to push too far. In a second or two, she'd probably lay down some ridiculous law, like I couldn't go to any camp at all, for the entire summer. I looked to Pippa for help.

"Um, I guess we could do Explorer's camp for a week or two," Pips said. "And then if Juliet's cooking camp is closer to home, maybe we can go to that all together?"

"Do you even want to do Explorer's camp?" I asked.

Just because Mom was freaking out right now, Pips shouldn't have to suffer with me.

"Actually, yes," Pips said, surprising me. "The kids are really amazing, and I did want to have time to do a week or two of camp with them this summer."

"What about Alice?" I asked.

"It's just a few weeks," Pips said. "It's not like we'd have all done camps together all summer anyway. We'll find something we can do as a group."

I couldn't ask the question I needed to ask Pips most, not with our moms here. What about Margo and their plan to stop her from winning the competition at design camp? Wouldn't everyone think I'd taken Pips away from them when they needed her? Especially once they found out what I really thought of their secret club?

Mom's face relaxed into a smile. "See, this is perfect. I'm sure you'll love Explorer's camp, Sadie."

"Can I at least go to the mall and the movies with the girls Thursday?" I asked.

Mom exchanged another look with Alexis before saying, "Let's talk to Dad about that."

"Seriously?" I had thought she'd give me an automatic yes.

"I just want to be careful, Sadie, that's all."

Before I could protest, Pippa squeezed my arm. I took the hint. Maybe Dad would be more reasonable.

"Ghirardelli anyone?" Pips asked, deliberately changing the subject the way she sometimes did.

No one could resist hot fudge sundaes, so we cleared our plates and used the GPS on Mom's phone to find the steps to Ghirardelli. The minute I saw the lighted arch, I asked for Mom's cell phone. It wasn't exactly a doorway, but close enough. I snapped a few pictures for reference. I could use white paint against a dark background to make the lights seem like they actually glowed.

Smells of cinnamon, vanilla, and chocolate tempted us as soon as we walked into the soda shop. We ordered two hot fudge sundaes to share—chocolate ice cream for Mom and I, vanilla for Pips and Alexis—a debate that had been going on for as long as I could remember, at least since Pips and I came to the city with our moms for the first time, when we were three. We argued about which was better all the way to our tables, and then sat down and dug in. Pips entertained us with sports blooper stories from the year, and as we laughed I almost was able to push thoughts of camp and Karl and Dad's case from my mind.

We ate every last bit of ice cream, and then bought chocolate squares for Dad, and more to send to Vivian, Ruth and Frankie, the assorted variety so they could try all the flavors. Pips remembered to grab a few samples for Jack.

We hurried back to the meeting place he'd suggested. He stood in his seat on the cart and waved us over.

"How was the afternoon?" he asked as we climbed in.

"Mostly good," Alexis said. "Full of food. I don't think any of us can eat another bite."

Jack laughed as he started pedaling. "No one goes home hungry from San Francisco. Where to, my friends?"

Mom gave Jack Dad's office address, and he started back down the Embarcadero.

Pips laced her arm through mine and whispered, "It will be okay, Sades."

I leaned back in my seat and tried to enjoy the ocean air, the sound of the seagulls, and the lingering taste of chocolate. Dad would understand that I couldn't be locked up all summer. Wouldn't he?

Chapter 6

Karl

Inside Dad's lobby, quiet jazz played and the fountain that spanned one entire wall gurgled calmly. When we'd come back from Owl Creek, Dad's old partners had invited him to come back to work with them, so he was back in this office building that I loved. On the main floor, past the front desk and bank of elevators, a small café served just about every flavor of juice you could imagine. And miniature cupcakes filled their glass cases, so small that Mom usually gave in and allowed me to have one.

"Please, Mom," Pippa begged. "Can we just run down to Bare Essentials super, super fast? It's right around the corner, and they have this new lip gloss—"

"Alexis, why don't you go," Mom said. "Sadie and I will go check on Matthew. I'm sure he'll take a few minutes to wrap up."

We checked in with the front desk attendant and clipped on visitor badges, while Pips literally bounced out the front door with Alexis.

On the elevator ride up, I searched my mind for some good argument, something to make Mom change her mind about camp. Dad worked up here in The City, so maybe he could drop us off for camp each morning. But then we'd have to arrive super early, which my parents probably wouldn't like. When we arrived on Dad's floor, I still hadn't come up with a workable plan.

No one was at the receptionist desk, but we knew the way back to Dad's office. Through the window, we saw him behind his desk, on the phone. He waved us in, and we sat on the plush couch that overlooked the Bay Bridge.

"Thank you, Greg," Dad said. "I agree. This will really help."

As he hung up, he gave us a big smile. "So, how was the adventure?"

"We had clam chowder, and watched the seals, and even brought you some chocolate," Mom said, handing the Ghirardelli bag over to Dad.

He riffled through and chose a Milk Chocolate Caramel, his favorite. "So, I was worried about nothing, I see."

"Well, a guy jumped out of the bushes at us," I said. "But it was just that crazy bush guy who thinks it's funny to scare people."

"And everything else is okay?" Dad asked, looking from Mom to me and back again.

He always knew when something was off.

"Matthew, don't worry," Mom said. "I'm feeling fine. Sadie's just upset because I don't want her to ride the train next week to The City for camp. I think it's too much, with your case and everything."

So much for coming up with the perfect argument before bringing this up with Dad. "We'd be all together, Dad. Pips, Alice, Bri, Juliet… Nothing could happen to us."

Mom didn't give Dad a chance to answer. "Alexis suggested that Pips and Sadie help out at the church camp for a few weeks until all of this blows over."

"So, if I don't go to design camp, Pips can't go either. It's so lame," I said.

Mom and Dad exchanged a look, and I knew in their minds the topic was closed. I picked up the glass paperweight off Dad's table and ran my fingers along the smooth edges. None of this was fair. I just wanted to breathe again. I wanted to wander around in the forest, or ride my bike up to Vivian's house, or go hiking in the snow with Andrew and Ruth. Wasn't hiking around hunters more dangerous than riding the train to the city?

"But you'll let me go to the mall and a movie with the girls Thursday, right?" I asked.

Mom opened her mouth to answer, but Dad said, "Actually, Sadie, there's something I want to talk to Mom about, which might solve this for all of us. Can you give us a minute or two to chat?"

I leapt on my opportunity. "If I can have a teeny-tiny cupcake?"

"After that hot-fudge sundae?" Mom shook her head. "How can you possibly be hungry?"

Dad passed me a ten-dollar bill. "Why don't you buy four to go, and we'll eat them for dessert later."

"Four?" I asked.

Dad winked at me. "Yep, four."

Well, something was going on. But I obviously wasn't going to have to wait forever to find out, if the cupcakes had something to do with it. I left them and mentally reviewed cupcake flavors as I rode the elevator down. Chocolate with vanilla frosting for Mom. Chocolate with double-fudge frosting for Dad. Vanilla with peanut butter frosting for me. And … vanilla with buttercream frosting for the mystery person?

I bought my cupcakes and took the little pink box back to the elevator. Right before the doors sealed, the bell dinged, and they began to open again. Maybe it was Pips and Alexis. Guiltily, I stared down at the box. I hadn't even thought of buying cupcakes for them. But when I looked up, I gasped. The doors were closing, trapping me in with crazy Karl.

He pushed the button for the very top floor and then moved in front of the button panel so I couldn't push Dad's floor. Why did I always wait for the last minute to do that? I shrank away from him, but I couldn't go far in the sleek, tiny elevator. Plus, the entire thing had mirrored walls, so wherever I looked, all I could see was his dark stare.

"Some things are just meant to be," Karl said. "It must be fate. Maybe you're the answer."

I couldn't speak.

"Look, Sadie." He stepped closer, reached out like he was going to grab my shoulder and then stopped, as though he'd thought better of it. "Sadie, you don't have a sister or brother, but you have a best friend. Pippa? Isn't that her name?"

Everything he said made my heart beat faster. How did he know Pips was my best friend? And what did he mean, I was the answer?

Karl looked over his shoulder to check the floor numbers. We were nearing the top, and he cursed under his breath. "Sadie, imagine Pippa got really sick, so sick you were sure she was going to die. And then, somehow, she survived. And years passed, and you started to forget all about the sickness. You started to feel like nothing could ever go wrong. Imagine then — "

The doors started to open, and he jabbed his finger against the "Close Doors" button. He could only hold the elevator here like this for a few seconds, maybe thirty, before the alarm started going off. And then what would he do?

He turned back to me with even more intensity, and I couldn't breathe. My heart pounded so loudly that I could barely hear his voice over the echo in my ears.

"Imagine then that Pippa died. No warning. And you had to live with it for the rest of your life. Wouldn't you want to keep other people from ever feeling that same pain?"

The elevator alarm started wailing.

"My sister — " Karl pressed his fist to his mouth, as though holding back a scream. He breathed for a moment and then leaned so close I could smell his cinnamon gum. "My sister died like that. That's why Tyler can't make this device all about testing kids. Once they're born, it's too late."

I couldn't press myself any further up against the mirrors. Karl couldn't stay here much longer before a security guard showed up. What would he do—grab me and drag me out with him? I'd started to crumple the edges of the cupcake box, my grip was so tight.

"Talk to your dad," Karl said. "Maybe he'll listen to you. Tell him the device has to test adults. It just has to. You understand, don't you?"

He let go of the button and grabbed my arm, his fingers hot on my skin. As the alarm stopped, the elevator doors opened. I nodded wildly. Anything to make him back off. Karl's entire body slackened, and he let go of my arm.

"Thank you." He pushed the button for Dad's floor before he left the elevator and stepped out onto the empty top floor. "Thank you, Sadie."

The doors slid closed, blocking him from my view. I sunk to the floor, my breath shaky and a little hysterical as I rode the elevator down.

Obviously, I had to tell Dad what had happened. But when I did, he would freak out more and make more rules, and possibly never let me be by myself, ever. I didn't want to see Karl again, but maybe now that he'd told me about his sister, now that I'd promised to talk to Dad, Karl would leave me alone.

When the elevator stopped on Dad's floor, I stood on

wobbly legs and peeked out of the elevator. No crazy Karl waiting. Right. Well, if the worst had already happened, there was no point in making my life more miserable by telling Dad. Not yet, anyway. I'd wait a bit. No harm in waiting, right? I could tell him eventually, after I heard about his solution, maybe. Maybe it would be a non-issue. He'd sounded positive on the phone when we came in. Maybe the case was almost over, and the fourth cupcake was for Tyler, to celebrate.

I smoothed the sides of the cupcake box the best I could on the way to Dad's office.

"There you are, Sadie," Dad said, coming over and giving me a sideways-squeeze. "I was beginning to think we'd lost you."

I smiled weakly.

"Pips and Alexis are waiting downstairs in the lobby," Mom said.

Dad shut off the lights and locked the doors, and I focused on breathing. In. Out. Everything would be okay. I watched the elevator lights scroll number by number through the floors. *Please don't let Karl suddenly appear.*

I probably shouldn't be praying for help when I was keeping a secret, a really, really big one, from Dad. The elevator pinged, and I gripped the cupcake box tighter. Empty. The elevator was empty.

"Sadie," Mom's voice was filled with concern. "Are you all right?"

I swallowed hard and willed my voice not to shake. "Yeah. I'm fine."

"You're not worried about Dad and my conversation are you?" she asked.

Good. Let her think all the new rules were the problem. I shrugged non-commitally.

"You'll have a wonderful summer." Mom pulled me close, and tears sprang to my eyes. "I promise. I know things haven't exactly been what you expected, but we'll work this out soon."

"And don't forget, I'm taking you girls waterskiing soon," Dad said. "That's something to look forward to."

In the lobby, Pips showed me her new lip-gloss, called "Cupcake," which made me feel better about my pink box.

"I need to tell you something later," I mouthed to her when Mom wasn't looking.

"Okay," she mouthed back.

Dad pulled the car around from the garage, and we all piled in. I ran my finger over the creases on my cupcake box. So, Karl's sister had died, unexpectedly, and like he said, it wasn't fair. It was never fair when kids died, or when anyone died, really. The only person I knew who had died was my great grandpa, and I'd only met him twice. I'd been three. So, I guess I didn't really understand how it felt to lose someone I loved. But was it normal to punch doorframes and curse years later? Karl was still so angry. I couldn't stop thinking about Karl's eyes. His sad, haunted look made me want to understand, even to help him somehow. But that was ridiculous, because why would I want to help someone who'd scared me to death, twice?

"Sadie . . ." Pips said, and I realized she'd said my name about five times already. "Are you okay?"

"Sorry, Pips," I said. "Yeah, I'm fine."

"So tell me about this door project," Pips said.

I smiled at her, grateful for the distraction, and we brainstormed places I might find interesting doors all the way down 101.

Chapter 7

In the Dark

During dinner, Mom and Dad discussed plans for a Hawaii trip later in the summer. I should have been excited, probably, but now that the fear and high-alert adrenaline from this afternoon had worn off, I felt drained.

Higgins put his paws on my lap and tried to slurp spaghetti off my plate. "Down, Hig."

He could tell I was half-hearted about pushing him down, and he could also tell I wasn't going to eat all my food. He was a mind reader like that.

"Hig!" Dad said, in his commanding voice.

Higgy dropped to the floor and laid his head on his paws, but jumped back onto his feet immediately when someone knocked on the door.

Dad broke into a smile. "Oh good, he's here. Time for

cupcakes. Now, Sadie, I want you to keep an open mind about this."

"About what?" I'd already had enough trouble for one day.

Dad headed for the door. "My boss offered to pay for someone to hang out with you for the next few weeks. That's what Mom and I talked about this afternoon."

He'd waited until the absolute last minute to mention this?

"What, like a nanny?" I called after him. "Are you serious? I'm turning thirteen this summer. And didn't you say he?"

I heard Dad open the door and then say, "Hi, Grant. Nice to meet you."

"Thank you." The man's voice was deep. Really deep.

"Come on in," Dad said.

The man who followed Dad into the kitchen was so tall his totally bald head almost touched the doorframe. He looked like he could lift a refrigerator over his head without breaking a sweat. A scar cut through the middle of his left eyebrow. He looked like the kind of person who might have a gun hidden somewhere on him, though he probably he wouldn't need it. One punch and anyone in his way was likely to be flat on the floor.

"Grant, this is Sadie, and my wife, Cindy."

Grant nodded at me. "Hi, Sadie. Cindy."

Mom looked just as speechless as I was.

"Um, hi?" I finally said.

"Grant will walk Higgins for us, and hang out with you, Sadie, when you go out. You wanted to go to the movies tomorrow, right?"

"Yeah, but . . ." I said.

"So, Grant can go with you," Dad said. "Do you know what time the girls are meeting?"

I blinked at Dad. "Four."

Mom found her voice. "Tomorrow morning, Sadie and I are going to First Episcopal to talk about Sadie and Pippa helping with summer camp."

"So sounds like we'll need you all day," Dad said. "Come around nine tomorrow?"

"Sure." Grant didn't crack a smile.

"Would you like a cupcake?" Dad asked, already on his way to the cupcake box.

Honestly? He was going to give the tiniest-ever cupcake to the hugest guy in the world?

Dad put cupcakes on plates and brought them to the table. Mom pulled out a chair. Grant sat and picked up his cupcake, angling it one way and another to try to take off the paper.

Mom laughed and offered to take it off for him. She seemed to have gotten over her shock. "These cupcakes are Sadie's favorite. What flavor is this, Sades?"

"Vanilla with butter cream frosting." My voice was little more than a croak.

Dad didn't actually think swat-guy was a solution, did he? Because hanging out with my friends with this guy hovering around would be worse than not hanging out at all. How could anything be normal with him there?

"A few things you should know . . ." Dad said, after

licking the extra frosting off his fingers. "The main trouble is with a man named Karl."

My heart stopped at the mention of his name. Panic pulsed through my body, and my fists clenched, hard. I should tell Dad. I should tell him now.

"Karl is determined to make the case I'm mediating an either-or," Dad said. "He'd like to force it into court so that he can win the jury's affection and convince them to rule in his favor."

"What's the argument?" Grant asked.

"My client, Tyler, invented a device with Karl, which tests for a genetic form of cancer that shows up in children. Probably, I should have expected the case to be emotional, because both men had siblings who died of this cancer at young ages. I just didn't foresee . . ."

"You couldn't have known, Matthew." Mom put her hand on his arm.

Dad ran his hand through his hair and continued. "Tyler would like the device to test children, who already have the gene. Karl is adamant that the test is tailored toward adults, potential parents, to discourage them from having children should the gene be present."

I stared at my uneaten cupcake, picturing Karl's face as he'd explained about his sister. If Karl wanted the case to go to court, I didn't doubt that it would. He wasn't the backing down kind.

"Karl is likely to push wherever he senses a weak point, and since he showed up here at the house and also followed

Sadie and Cindy to the beach the other day, I'd rather not take any chances."

Dad's words hung in the air, and I wondered what he meant by chances. What did he think Karl might do? After today, I was pretty sure he didn't plan to kidnap me, but who knew? If he thought it might help with the case, I wasn't sure he'd stop at anything.

"Anything else?" Grant asked.

"Mostly, I just want to keep the case as far away from Sadie and Cindy as possible. They've been through enough already."

Grant shook Dad's hand. "I'll keep my eyes open. And I'll plan to be here at nine tomorrow morning."

After Dad walked Grant to the door, he nearly bounced back to the table, grinning.

"He'll do, won't he?"

"He looks like he should be on a swat team," I said. "What am I supposed to tell the girls? Here's Grant, he's my bodyguard?"

Dad winked at me. "You could call him your nanny. Or maybe your manny?"

I felt my eyebrows almost lift off my face. "Dad, that isn't funny."

Dad put his hand on my shoulder. "Grant is perfect. It's only for a little while, I promise."

"You're ruining my life." When I said this, heard my accusation out loud, I realized how much I blamed Dad for everything that was going wrong. If it weren't for his dumb case, I wouldn't be in danger in the first place.

"Sadie, you're overreacting. No one will care if Grant chaperones you for a while."

Showed how much he knew. I tried to lower my voice, to sound calm and reasonable. "Please, Dad. Don't do this."

"Sadie, I promise when this is all over, you'll get your freedom back. I'm only asking you to be patient for a little while. I don't think this case will go on for all that long."

But while I was being patient, my life was becoming a disaster. My friends wouldn't wait forever. Still, I could see from their faces that nothing I said would make any difference.

Inside my head I ranted and raved and threw a fit while I cleared my plate and took Higgy upstairs. Andrew probably still hadn't written me, but now I really had to email him. He'd know what to do about Dad hiring a body builder to be my nanny. And I could tell him the truth about what happened today and trust him not to tell anyone else. I waited for my email to load and started typing before I had time to chicken out.

From: Sadie Douglas
To: Andrew Baxter
Date: Wednesday, June 8, 8:27 pm
Subject: Swat-dude

So my dad hired this guy who looks like a navy seal to be my
nanny aka bodyguard. Okay, back up. Here's what's going on.
Dad's new case is going haywire and one of the guys he's working with followed Mom and I to the beach, and he showed up
at the house to shout at Dad, and then today he cornered me
in the elevator at Dad's work. He told me why he needs to win
the case my dad is working on — it's a long story — and now I
don't know what to do. I was really freaked out in the elevator,
but in the end, this guy didn't do anything to me. And if I tell
Dad about the elevator, he'll just lock me down further, and
maybe not even let me leave the house. And now, if swat dude
is around, there's nothing to really worry about, right?

What do you think I should do?

Sorry… that was all about me. How are you?

71

From: Sadie Douglas
To: Frankie Paulson
Date: Thursday, June 9, 8:35 pm
Subject: RE: Tree House Door

I love your collage of the Tree House door. Are you going to collage all of your images? I really like how it turned out, especially because in the photo the different papers look like they have different textures. I wish I could touch them.

I hadn't thought about doing a series of images to show a doorway, or about finding objects that weren't anything like doorways and making them appear to be doors. Vivian is so smart. :-) Tell her thanks for me. Now I have a bunch of new ideas.

I painted my first door last night, one I found on my trip to The City. Since it's dry now, I can put it in the mail tomorrow. And I have a present for you and Vivian, too!

Chapter 8

Jess

Grant drove Mom, Pips, and me to the church in his Hummer, which felt like driving across town in an armored truck. I'd never been so grateful for tinted windows. After I begged and begged, Grant agreed to wait outside while Mom walked us in. I guess he decided nothing bad could happen inside the church.

As we walked into the foyer, I took a deep breath. The church smelled familiar—like lemon polish from Ruth's church, plus incense like Vivian's cathedral, mixed with a hint of cinnamon, like the Tree House where we held youth group. It wasn't always cinnamon, but Doug and Penny, our youth group leaders, always baked something yummy for our meetings.

Inside the sanctuary, a lady who looked about Penny's age, but nothing like Penny called hello and wound her way through the pews to meet us. Instead of Penny's spiky, purple hair and funky clothes, she wore jeans, a t-shirt, and flip-flops, and her straight ash-blonde hair looked like she'd never dyed it in her life. Still, the two had a similar feel to them, comfortable, settled, in a way I hoped I'd be someday.

She held out her hand to Mom. "I'm Jess, Mrs. Douglas. Very nice to meet you." When she turned to me, she grinned. "And Sadie. I've heard so much about you."

She slipped an arm around Pippa's shoulders and squeezed her tight.

"Pippa told us all about Explorer's camp, and we'd so appreciate you allowing the girls to help," Mom said. "It's an unusual summer for us, and I'd rather the girls didn't have to sit around home. This way, they can spend time together, and do something helpful besides."

It had been a long time since Mom had spoken for me; trying to sell me on something I was only half interested in doing. But a tiny part of me loved that Mom was back, doing Mom things, even if they were all the wrong things.

Jess smiled at me, like she could see straight into my mind. "Why don't you girls come to my office and we can chat. Would you like a cup of coffee, Mrs. Douglas?"

"Call me Cindy," Mom said. "I may just pop around the corner to the bookstore. Will you be a few minutes?"

"Maybe half an hour," Jess said. "I'll show the girls around and give them the low-down."

Mom pushed through the double doors and followed Grant to the Hummer. Well, there was one good thing about Grant. He'd look out for Mom when Dad and I couldn't.

Whenever Mom went somewhere by herself, I couldn't help worrying that would be the day she'd push too far and collapse, alone, in a store or a coffee shop.

"She's looking really healthy," Jess said, as we followed her back into the office. "Pips and I prayed together for her as she was struggling so much with her health."

I nodded and found myself talking to Jess before I stopped to consider that she was still a stranger. "She's been taking new vitamins, but mostly, she's just not so depressed. I think she was ... I don't know ... trying too hard to pretend she was okay. For me. And it wore her out."

"Well, it sounds like now she's saving energy, for what she really wants to do," Jess said. "Like spending time with you."

As Jess opened her office door, she smiled at Pips. "Pippa, you're quiet today. Everything all right?"

"Yeah. I guess. Alice and I argued on the phone this morning. She's upset about Sadie and me doing this camp."

"Change is always hard," Jess said. "And no one likes feeling left out, no matter the circumstances."

"I'm not trying to leave her out." Pips flopped onto the couch. "I invited her to come too."

"But you do understand why she feels uncomfortable, too," Jess reminded Pips gently. "One of the most hurtful things we can do when we have big differences from our friends is to pretend those differences don't exist. Friendship requires honesty, even when it's hard."

Pips groaned and leaned her head back against the cushion. "Why can't it just be easy?"

Jess laughed, a kind laugh, the type that makes you feel like everything will turn out okay. "Why don't you sit down too, Sadie."

I sat by Pips, and Jess sat in an armchair across from us. The desk was against the wall, but this part of the room was almost like a living room. I scanned the bookshelves. Jess had Bibles and a whole section of serious-looking books with leather covers and gold on their spines. But then she also had two shelves stuffed full of picture books.

"So, what has Pips told you about our kids?" Jess asked.

"Not a lot," I said. "Just that the camp is for little kids and we'll be teaching art."

Jess took out a notebook and flipped it open. "Yep, true on both counts. Our church population has always been a little unique. We're very close to Stanford hospital, and maybe as much as a fourth of our congregation is made up of families staying in town for a little while—three months, six months, eight months, while a relative receives specialized care."

She passed the notebook across and I flipped through the pages, which each had a picture of a camper with contact information and some notes. They were all so young. I didn't know anything about little kids. I'd been around Ruth's brother and sister, but she was always the one to wipe their drippy noses, or calm them down when they cried.

Pips leaned over my shoulder. "That's Fritz. He wears a cape every day and insists he can turn invisible whenever he wants."

"His dad is a physics professor at Stanford," Jess said. "No sickness in his family, just pure creativity."

Okay, I had to admit, a kid who wore a cape was kind of cool. I turned the page.

"And Isabel," Jess said. "She hasn't spoken to me once since she started attending Sunday school three months ago. I'm hoping camp opens her up a little. Her mom just had a heart transplant and she and her dad live in a studio apartment right down the road."

Pips touched the next page. "Charlotte's coming to camp?"

"Yes," Jess said. "And I'm so glad because it will help distract her while Cici is in quarantine, going through chemo."

"They're Tyler's daughters," Pippa told me.

"Wait. Tyler's daughter has cancer?" Last night Dad said Tyler's sibling died of this cancer, but his daughter too?

"Childhood cancer runs in Tyler's family," Jess said. "He's been through so much."

"Cici and Charlotte are twins," Pippa said. "And super close. Sometimes I find Charlotte in the book corner reading out loud, and she tells me Cici is listening."

Dad must not know that Tyler's daughter was attending camp. He wanted me as far away from the case as possible, so he'd probably hate this. But Charlotte's expression drew me in, the way her blue eyes twinkled, like she'd just thought of an idea she couldn't wait to share.

"Those two girls have such a strong connection," Jess said. "And ripping them apart has been hard on the whole family."

We flipped through the rest of the pages, and my confidence swung up and down. One minute, I thought I could be like Vivian, opening a new door for a kid who'd never really drawn anything before. And the next, their stories depressed me. The kids weren't old enough for these kinds of problems.

"It sounds sad," Pips said to me, reading the worry on my face. "But you'll see. The minute you meet them, you'll see they're just kids. Wild, crazy kids. You'll love them."

"Wild is right." Jess stood up. "Let me show you the art room."

We walked down a long hall to a room with lots of windows that overlooked a grove of redwood trees. Tables and chairs to hold about twenty kids filled the space, and counters lined the walls, overflowing with art supplies. More importantly, it smelled like art, like chalk and pastels and paint. In front of the tables, there was a carpet area and a screen.

"That's a smart board," Jess said, motioning to the screen. "We have lots of technology here if you want it. You can draw directly on the board, or display artwork, or whatever you like."

"So we'll teach art every morning?" Pips asked. "For how long?"

"The kids are with us all day, so there's no rush, but we should think about their attention span. I think an hour would work, between explaining, making the art, and sharing it," Jess said.

"What do they do for the rest of camp?" I asked.

"Each afternoon, we throw together an impromptu play to perform for parents just before dismissal."

I circled the room, looking over the paintbrushes and paper and materials as I listened. Jess went on, "We have chapel each morning with singing and a lesson. And centers too, so the kids have choices—cooking, sewing, reading, outside free play."

"So, Sades?" Pips asked as we followed Jess out of the art room. "Want to give it a try?"

Pips seemed so comfortable with this, even eager. I'd never seen her around little kids before, so it was strange to see this new part of her. Yet another reminder of how much we had both changed this year.

"What kind of art do you want us to do?" I asked Jess.

"It's up to you—different projects for each day, or maybe one longer project, or some combination of the two. We have a bookmaking machine, if you decide you want to have the kids make picture books."

"I've never really taught kids before," I said.

Jess laughed. "Pippa is great with the kids. Between your art skills and Pippa's charm, you'll be fine. And I'll be with you the whole time, helping, so you won't be on your own."

No of course not. Because I'd never be on my own again, ever. Now I had Grant. I knew that wasn't what Jess had meant, but I couldn't help sighing anyway.

Jess put an arm around Pips and me. "You'll both be great."

Something else was bothering me too. "And, um … What about the church thing? Are we supposed to, I don't know, make art about Bible stories or things like that?"

Pippa groaned. "Now you're starting to sound like Alice."

"Hey, Pips," Jess said. "It's a fair question. Sadie, I want you to be yourself. Does God ever come up when you draw or paint on your own?"

"Yeah," I said. "But not because I'm drawing Moses, or anything like that. It's more like my art helps me see God better. But I'm not sure I could explain the connection to six-year-olds. I can hardly explain it to Pips."

Pippa rolled her eyes at me. "You should hear her talk about her paintings, Jess."

"I'd love that," Jess said. "Sadie, for now, why don't you and Pippa choose projects that will spark the kids' creativity. I'll bet, in the process, moments will arise for you to talk about your own experience with art and God. I'll pray for those moments to arise, in fact."

My mouth went dry and my panic must have shown on my face, because Pippa elbowed me and grinned. "Sadie, you'll be okay."

I swallowed hard. "Easy for you to say."

Jess laughed. "The kids are going to love working with you two."

"So now, all we have to do is come up with a lesson," Pips said, as we walked into the foyer where Mom waited with Grant.

Jess went still, staring up at him, her expression similar

to Mom's last night. Amazement, shock, and maybe a little fear. He was just so ... big.

"Grant, meet Jess," Mom said. "Grant will be dropping off the girls and picking them up."

"Uh, okay," Jess said, still looking up at Grant.

Grant held out his huge hand. "Nice to meet you."

Jess shook it, smiling weakly. "Nice to meet you too, Grant."

"How'd it go, girls?" Mom asked as we walked out to the Hummer.

"I'm not sure ... " I said.

Pips swatted at me. "Just wait until you meet the kids. We'll be fine, I promise."

Maybe. Or maybe if the kids got too out of control, Fritz could teach me his turning-invisible trick. But as I got into the Hummer, my excitement was winning out over my worry. Charlotte's smile, that full-of-ideas expression, made me want to come up with the perfect project for them. Maybe this wouldn't be so bad after all.

From: Sadie Douglas
To: Ruth Manning
Date: Wednesday, June 8, 1:45 pm
Subject: He wrote me!!

I wrote to Andrew about the new nanny my dad got me, who's more like a navy seal. And I know you won't like this, because you don't like it when I keep secrets, but one of the guys Dad is working with cornered me on an elevator at Dad's work and told me I had to convince Dad to listen to his point of view about the case. I didn't tell Dad because he's already so freaked out about this guy that he won't let me go anywhere on my own. And now that I have Grant following me everywhere, maybe it's not worth worrying Dad. Plus, if I tell him now, he'll be so mad that I didn't say something right away, I don't know what to do. It's all a huge mess.

BUT! Andrew wrote me back. Here's what he said:

Good to hear from you, Sades. But I'm worried. You should tell your parents about this guy, even if you do have swat-dude following you around. I don't want anything to happen to you. Everyone here is doing well, and the bears and the cubs are all good. It's not the same without you, though.

I know you probably agree with him that I should tell Dad. I will... soon. But I had to show you Andrew's note, especially the end part. It's good, right? The "it's not the same without you" bit? This is really, really hard, Ruth. I miss him. I miss you too. Send news.

Chapter 9

The Plan

Bri took the tank top out of Juliet's hands. "Focus, Juliet. Design camp?"

Juliet snatched it back. "If I'm going to design camp I need this tank top. I'm not going in ratty old clothes."

"Sadie and I are skipping out on this one," Pips said. "But we'll come to the show on Friday night and do whatever."

I hadn't worked up the guts to tell her I didn't want to be a part of the bullying scheme. And here I was, right in the middle of the planning process. So far, the girls were brainstorming how to make sure Margo didn't sabotage the competition.

Bri glanced over her shoulder at Grant, who leaned against a nearby wall. "Why, doesn't the Incredible Hulk want to come to design camp?"

I picked at my fingernail while everyone else laughed.

Bri swatted my shoulder. "Oh, come on, Sadie. I'm only joking. It's kind of cool to have our own personal superhero."

Alice motioned us all closer and lowered her voice. "Okay. Just make sure he doesn't hear us talking about the plan."

Juliet shook her head. "Alice, you're so cloak and dagger about this. What's the big deal?"

"We could get in huge trouble," Alice said. "You all know that."

"We're not doing anything wrong," Bri said, and then her eyes went wide. "No way."

"What?" we all asked.

"No way," she repeated. "Margo."

We turned to look where she was staring. A super-skinny girl with long blond hair, designer jeans, and too much eyeliner had just walked into the store.

She smirked and sauntered over to us. "You're not going to buy that tank top, are you, Juliet? Because sleeveless isn't your style."

She leaned in to whisper, "Arm flab, you know."

Juliet's cheeks flamed and I wanted to punch Margo right then and there. Margo gave us a smooth smile and riffled through the bin of sale jewelry.

"They sell such junk in this store. And then, they put security tags on all of it. Honestly. Like anyone would want to steal it." She looked pointedly into Bri's purse and then gave a huge, fake gasp of surprise.

She raised her voice so everyone in the store could hear

her next words. "You wouldn't actually steal those, would you, Brianna?"

Margo smiled triumphantly as the salesgirl bustled in our direction. "See ya, girls."

Bri hastily pulled the earrings out of her purse, but not before the salesgirl saw her. "I'm sorry, but—"

Grant closed the distance between us almost immediately. "The girl who was just here dropped those into Bri's purse."

The salesgirl looked up at Grant with the half-terrified look almost everyone gave him. She cleared her throat. "Are you ... um ... sure?"

"Positive," Grant said.

"Uh, well, okay," the salesgirl said. "Just, uh, let me know if you need help."

Maybe having Grant around wasn't all that bad.

"Thanks," Bri said to Grant, as the salesgirl left.

"Are you girls ready to go?" Grant asked.

"Just a few more minutes?" No way would I let Juliet leave without buying the tank top now. "Juliet wants to try on that tank top."

Once Grant was out of earshot, Alice whispered, "See? She's terrible."

The thing was, Alice was right. Margo was terrible. But still, ganging up on her was wrong. I should say something. I knew I should. But what?

"So are we going to try these on?" Alice asked Juliet. "I think we should get matching ones for camp. You too, Bri."

Alice had a lot of difficult qualities. She was bossy and opinionated and sometimes she pouted when she didn't get her way. But she was also a totally loyal friend.

Juliet shrugged, totally unconvincingly. We all knew Margo had gotten under her skin.

"Come on, Juliet," Bri said, choosing a matching tank top off the rack, and she and Alice marched Juliet off to the dressing room.

Pips and I looked through the jewelry and hair glitz at the front of the store while we waited for the girls.

"You should get these, Sadie." Pippa held up a pair of bobby pins, each with stars. "They'd match your necklace and earrings."

Without thinking, I reached for my earring. Andrew. He popped into my mind when I least expected, and every time, that little thrill of pain—or was it happiness—shot through me.

Pippa put the bobby pins in my hand and closed my fingers around them. "Come on, you know you want to."

Her face went pale, and I followed her gaze out the store window. Two boys stood outside. I thought I recognized them from her pictures.

"Isn't that Ryan?" I asked.

The other boy saluted Pips.

"And Rickey," she said, waving. "Juliet is going to hate this. I told Ryan we were going to the mall and a movie, but I didn't think he'd show up. I'll go talk to him."

Pips went outside and Grant walked over to me. "Busy night."

"That's Pippa's friend who's a boy," I said. "She wants to invite him to the movie."

Grant shrugged. "I'll chaperone."

I'd expected Grant to be humiliating, but so far, he'd only been helpful.

"I'll go call her mom to make sure it's okay." Grant walked out to talk to Pips.

"What's going on?" Alice asked, back from the dressing rooms with Bri and Juliet.

"That better not be Rickey out there." Juliet glared out the window.

The girls paid for their tank tops, and I bought the bobby pins, and then we all went out to join Pips and the boys. Grant hung up from his conversation with Alexis.

"You guys can come along if you want," he said to the boys.

Rickey looked like he wanted to make a snide comment, but he must have thought better of it. He took one look at Grant and closed his mouth.

"We better go if we want to buy popcorn and sour patch kids." Pippa checked her watch.

"Is Jason coming?" Bri asked Ryan.

Ryan leaned back on his heels and smiled, a good smile that made me instantly like him. He had wavy brown hair that he wore a little long, and the freckles on his nose matched Pippa's.

"I called him, but he wasn't super excited about the girly movie," Ryan said.

"Sour Patch Kids?" Pips had already started walking. "I can't watch a movie without them."

The movie theatre was at the other end of the mall. When we finally arrived, and after we waited through the endless ticket line, Pips led us to the candy counter.

"Want some worms, Juliet?" Rickey asked.

She brushed past him and went for a soda. Apparently, her strategy was "pretend he's not here." The rest of us loaded up on popcorn and candy, and then we searched for our theatre.

Grant sat a few rows behind us to give us a little space. Pips, Ryan, and Rickey shared a bucket of popcorn, and the other girls had a bucket too. No big deal, it wasn't like they meant to leave me out. Still, every tiny lonely moment felt like a big deal, just now. I wished Andrew were here. Or even Ruth or Frankie. But the only person I had was my super-nanny. Grant's watchful eyes burned into the back of my head. I slumped down in my seat and pretended to be very interested in choosing Jelly Belly flavors until the lights lowered.

All I had to do was survive the movie. Afterwards, we'd take the girls home, and I could go draw. I wished I could bring my sketchbook with me everywhere, so that even here, in the dark, I could draw when I needed to. But sketching at a movie would only prove how different from the others I was, and right now I felt alien enough.

A pack of boy-crazy girls chased a superhero across the screen, squealing.

"I bet Grant's loving that," I said.

Pips snorted. "I'm sure he loves squealing."

I threw a smile back at him, and I swear he smiled back. So. Swat-guy could smile.

From: Sadie Douglas
To: Frankie Paulson
Date: Friday, June 10, 6:15 pm
Subject: RE: Bird House Doors

Nice! I liked both Vivian and your pictures of the birdhouse doors. I didn't know Ms. Rose had a birdhouse collection. Feeding birds is better than feeding bears, right? On your collage it looked like the wings were three dimensional off the page. Is that true? What did you make them out of? Will they pop up when someone turns to that page in the sketchbook?

Today was the most boring day ever. I want to go find a door, but I'm not allowed out of my house without my new nanny, aka bodyguard, and he's off today. Long story. Tomorrow he's coming over to walk Higgins, so I can at least go out then. I miss you! Keep sending drawings.

Chapter 10

Confidential

Dad was working at home today, and Grant was over to walk Higgins, so the kitchen was crowded at lunch. Mom, Dad, Grant, and I sat at the table eating sandwiches. Higgins chowed down on a rawhide bone, since technically he only ate breakfast and dinner.

I ripped off some lettuce and nibbled, wondering how to make Grant smile again. Yesterday at the movies, he'd seemed almost human. If I could make him smile in front of my parents, that would be a true victory.

While I was still weighing options, Dad's cell phone rang. He made an apologetic face and pushed back in his chair.

"I'm sorry, who is this?" After listening for a moment, he shook his head. "No. I have no statement. The case is confidential."

Anger tightened at the corner of his lips as he continued to listen.

"I'm sorry to hear that. No. I have no public statement." He hung up, put the phone back into his pocket, and took his nearly uneaten sandwich to the sink.

"Where are you going?" Mom asked.

"I need to go back to the office," Dad said. "Grant, can you please stay tonight until I'm home? It may be after dinner. Call for take out or something, Cindy. And save me some, please."

He kissed her on the top of her head, grabbed an apple and headed for the door, not looking at me once. I twisted my napkin, trying to keep my face neutral. He couldn't know about the elevator, could he? I hadn't even thought about possible security tapes. Someone could have seen Karl and said something to Dad. Was that why he was hurrying off to work?

"Wait, Matthew," Mom said. "Who was that? What did they want?"

I couldn't look at him, could hardly breathe.

But Dad only sighed. "I'll tell you when I get home. It's a mess."

The kitchen door swung behind him and he was gone.

Grant picked up his sandwich, which, like everything, looked miniature in his huge hands. "I'll pick up food later."

I smoothed out my napkin. Like I could eat after all that.

"Not hungry, Sadie?" Mom asked.

"May I be excused?" I asked.

She nodded, and I went upstairs to wait for Grant to finish eating. I flopped onto my bed and closed my eyes.

I'm scared.

The prayer, which was not much of a prayer, came out sharp and surprising. Everything had been happening so fast and I hadn't taken time to be quiet, to pray. For me, the best way to quiet my mind and talk with God was to draw. Last year, no matter how bad things became, drawing had been my anchor. I'd begun to need to draw the way I needed to breathe. The smell of charcoal and the sound of stroke after stroke on paper calmed me until I could gather all my questions and thoughts and worries, and dump them all out on the page, so I could see them clearly. And as I did, tiny thoughts slipped into my mind, thoughts I hadn't considered before. They calmed me and helped me see myself and even the rest of the world differently. Maybe I couldn't hear God's voice, exactly, but I'd begun to recognize these thoughts, the tone and feeling of them, and knew they were from God.

Drawing this way, opening up, was scary, too. I'd likely learn the truth about my feelings, even truths I had hidden from myself. Like my prayer. I'd been working too hard to cover up my secrets; I hadn't admitted to myself that I was scared, too.

I took out my sketchbook and drew quickly, little snippets of whatever flashed to mind: Andrew throwing a stick into the creek for Sink-the-Boat, Pippa running on the beach, Ruth eating ice cream at Black Bear Java, Vivian adding ceramics to one of her sculptures. I wasn't afraid of any of these things, so why were these images coming to mind, instead of Karl, or Dad totally furious with me? Maybe I was afraid I'd never be happy like that again. My life would continue to get worse and worse, like a bad movie, with Grant, the muscle man, shadowing me everywhere I went. Dad, in the middle of huge trouble at work. Me, hiding a million secrets that weren't entirely my fault, while trying to fit back into my life here. Deep down, I knew I'd have to eventually tell Dad about Karl, or he'd find out on his own. He'd find out about Charlotte and camp, too. And I'd be grounded for life, locked up in my house with my sick mom and the bodyguard.

"Ready, Sadie?" Grant called up to me.

When I came downstairs, he already had Higgins leashed up and ready to go.

Mom stood in the hallway, nervously straightening the pictures on the wall. "If you see anyone suspicious, call me right away."

"Okay, Mom," I said. "But you're not supposed to answer the phone."

Mom fluttered her hand impatiently. "I can answer if it's Grant's number. And keep your eyes open, Sadie."

"I will."

Mom gave me a once over. "Maybe you shouldn't go today. Should I call Dad and ask?"

"Mom, I need air. You can't keep me cooped up inside all the time. And I'll be with Grant. And Higgins."

"We'll be all right," Grant said. "I promise. See you in about half an hour, Cindy."

Higgins took off the minute Grant opened the door, and I nearly had to run to keep up with them. We turned left out of the driveway and lurched along the wide embankment between the two-lane road and the redwood forest as Higgins darted after every squirrel. Our house wasn't really in a neighborhood. Woodside was more like a forest that had been tamed every half-mile or so to allow for a house.

"Did anyone train him?" Grant asked as Higgins yanked his arm yet again.

"He grew up in a real forest, and I gave up on leashing him. He's addicted to squirrels."

"I see that," Grant said, his elusive smile playing at the edges of his mouth.

He tugged on the leash. "Sit, Higgins."

Higgins sat, immediately, and I stared, "How did you do that?"

"Here, you take the leash." Grant handed over the leash and traded me places. "Stand on his right, and give him a little slack with his leash. If it's tight, he'll always pull."

I let the leash out a bit.

"Now say, 'heel,' and start walking. The minute he pulls, stop, and make him sit again."

I took two steps and Higgins was already tugging at the end of his leash. "He doesn't know this command."

"No, but he'll learn. As you go, give the leash little tugs

and remind him to heel. When he walks beside you, give him a treat." Grant passed me a handful of small treats.

I started up again, tugging and telling Higgy to heel. The second he started prancing along beside me, I laid on the encouragement thick, telling him what a good dog he was and gave him a treat. He tilted his head and cocked an ear, his classic are-you-nuts look. We started up again, and he heeled for a good fifteen seconds. I gave him another treat.

"He's smiling at you," Grant said. "And catching on."

We did the heel-treat thing until my treats were gone and my arm muscles ached.

"Okay, your turn." I handed the leash back to Grant.

Higgins was far from a perfect walker, and he lost focus every time something rustled in the underbrush, but at least I could keep up with him and Grant now. If only every problem were as easy to solve. I felt like I might explode with all the secrets building up inside me, knowing that Dad might come home totally furious. Still, I wasn't ready to talk about Karl. Maybe if I talked to Grant about one of my other million problems, I'd start to get a grip.

"What do you think of Margo?" I asked, the question nearly bursting out of me. "You know, the girl who dropped the earrings in Bri's purse?"

After a pause, Grant said, "She's angry about something."

I stopped walking. "Why do you say that?"

"You can tell by the way she stands, the way she walks. Like with Higgins. You can see stubbornness in his body

95

language. He clearly wants to do things his own way, but he also wants to please. All this heeling and giving treats wouldn't work if Higgins were angry. We'd have to train him a totally different way."

There was no way that the solution to fixing Margo was like training a dog.

Still, I couldn't help asking, "So, uh … how would you train a dog if it were angry?"

"First you'd have to convince the dog you were a friend," Grant said.

All I could think about was Karl. "Can I tell you something?"

Grant didn't answer. He just looked at me, waiting for whatever I would say.

I chickened out. "My friends do this thing where they try to stop people like Margo from pushing them around, by intimidating them or threatening them. And I know it's wrong, what my friends are doing, but I can't ask them to sit back and let Margo treat them like that, either."

Grant nodded, and when he didn't offer advice, I started walking again. It felt good to talk, even if I wasn't telling him about Karl.

"In Owl Creek, this girl, Frankie, picked on me from the minute I arrived for no good reason. But like you said, she was super angry about a lot of things that mostly didn't have to do with me. And after a while, a long couple months, she and I started to work things out."

Grant had Higgins totally under control as we walked side by side. "What changed?"

"Her dad forced her to pretend to be my friend, but while she was pretending, we actually got to know one another, and we realized we'd made unfair assumptions about each other. And then, when the truth came out about her dad, we had to learn how to trust one another."

"Not everyone can end up friends in the end, though," Grant said.

"No." I kicked a pinecone out of the path. "I can't imagine Juliet and Margo becoming friends."

"Still, mutual respect might be possible."

I nodded, tucking this away to think about later. Maybe it was possible to find a solution that didn't involve ganging up on Margo. I could try to figure one out at least. And maybe eventually, Dad could help Tyler and Karl find some mutual respect, too.

I looked across the road at the giant house coming up on our right, white pillars and all. I'd almost forgotten to look for doors. Not that door, though. Too stuffy.

A small winding road led off to our left, lined with smaller houses that looked like cabins and giant redwood trees.

"Can we go that way?" I asked.

Grant glanced up the road, probably assessing risk. Then, he gave a small nod and turned. Somewhere, one of these houses had to have a door worth painting. I'd even settle for a creaky old gate as long as it was interesting. And had good texture. With paint, texture mattered.

We rounded a corner and there, tucked into the trees, was a house entirely covered in ivy. The door had been painted red once, but now was weatherworn and peeling. I stopped and stared.

Grant stopped a hundred yards beyond me, realizing I wasn't with him. "What?"

"Can I borrow your phone?"

He hurried back. "Do you see something?"

"No, I just need a picture of that door. Tell me a family of dwarves doesn't live there."

Grant looked at me like I'd grown an extra ear. "A family of what?"

"Never mind. So can I borrow your phone?"

He handed it over and I snapped a picture of the door.

Grant checked his watch. "We should start back, so your mom doesn't worry."

Okay by me. Now that I'd found the door, I couldn't wait to dip my brush into paint.

"You take Higgins again," Grant said. "It's good practice."

From: Sadie Douglas
To: Andrew Baxter
Date: Sunday, June 12, 4:45 pm
Subject: You're right…

Sorry, Andrew. I should have emailed you right back. Yes. I promise I'll tell Dad. I will. Soon.

Tomorrow, I start teaching at this camp for little kids. Pips and I are leading the art lessons. Don't laugh. I have no idea how I'll do with the kids. There's this girl attending camp, Charlotte, who's actually the daughter of my dad's client. If Dad knew, he'd probably tell me not to teach. He wants me as far away from his case as I can be. But every time I turn around, every-where I go, people from his case show up. I can't help it. And even though I'm nervous about camp, I'd rather teach art with Pips than sit at home, which is my only other option.

I know. I need to tell Dad. The thing is, maybe if I've already started camp, he won't force me to stop.

And you! Wow. Big news. I didn't know you were interested in wolves. How does your mom feel about you going away for a year? How did you meet this biologist? What will you do at the Wolf Center? When will you go?

Chapter 11

Bouncing Off the Walls

I had never seen so many kids before in my life. Okay maybe that was an exaggeration. Still, there were literally kids everywhere, bouncing off the walls, drawing self portraits on the tables, and playing some form of crawl-tag under the tables.

"Oh good, you're here," Jess said. "The natives are getting restless."

I scanned the room. I was supposed to teach these kids how to draw? How was that even possible?

"Beetle," Jess called over the din.

Suddenly, amazingly, they all stopped, turned to her, and shouted, "Face!"

They all made crazy faces with fingers wiggling like antennae for about ten seconds and then dropped obediently into chairs, as though they were the best behaved group of kids you've ever seen.

Jess grinned. "Impressive. Ten more beetle-faces like that and you'll win your Popsicle party."

"Who're they?" asked a boy whose cheeks were still streaked with chalk from making self-portraits.

"These are our art teachers," Jess said. "Miss Sadie and Miss Pippa."

"But I'm more of a helper than a teacher," Pips chimed in.

Right. Like I was the teacher of the two of us.

"Today you're going to make a drawing that tells us a little about you," Pips used the smart board pens to draw a simple example. She started with a curved v to represent a bird. "If I could be any kind of animal, I'd be a bird. I like to see everything and know everything that is going on, so I know I'd love to fly. If my bird could live anywhere, she would live at the beach." Pips added a scalloped wave to the bottom of the picture, and then handed me the pen. "My friends would all be good at different things. Sadie, can you draw a crab and an otter?"

Right. Put *me* on the spot for the hard part. I drew a rough outline of an otter on its back, and added a rock for the crab to lounge on.

Pips went on. "The otter would make me laugh, and the crab would help us gather food with his pinchers."

Kids hands shot up all across the room.

"I'd be a giraffe because I want to be taller than everyone else. But I'd have a mouse friend who sat on my head, so she'd really be the tallest of all. I'd help her."

"I'd be a dog and I'd be good at all kinds of tricks. And

I'd work at a library so I could go fetch all the books that people wanted."

"I'd be a kangaroo who hopped higher than anyone on the trampoline. And I'd join the circus."

How did they think of these things? I took out paper and pencils. No need for me to show more examples. There were ready to go.

"But I don't know how to draw an elephant," a little girl with two bright red pigtails said.

To tell the truth, I'd have a hard time drawing an elephant off the top of my head. "Um ..." And then I remembered the shelves of picture books Jess had shown us in her office.

"Jess, could we borrow some of your picture books?"

"Sure. I'll go get some." She hurried out, leaving us alone with the kids.

It was fine. We'd be fine. Pips gave me an encouraging look, and I tried to smile back.

I cleared the smart board page. "You can look in the books for examples of the animals you want to draw. Then, look for the main shapes. For instance, an elephant needs a big round body ..." I drew an oval, and then added to my picture as I explained. "You'd need four rectangle legs, and a roundish head, and a rope-like tail."

"What about the ears?" As soon as I saw his cape, I knew he must be Fritz.

I held up my pen, and then paused. I didn't want to admit I had no idea how to draw the ears, but I probably couldn't stall until Jess returned with the books.

"You know what," I said finally. "I can't picture the ears. That's why the books are so helpful. When Jess gets back, I'll find an elephant picture and add ears."

One of the girls smiled shyly at me. I think she was Isabel, the girl Jess said never spoke. Maybe admitting I didn't know everything wasn't the worst thing in the world.

Pips and I passed out paper and distributed cups of colored pencils, and just as all the kids were settled, Jess came back with books.

"Miss Sadie," the little girl with pigtails called. "Help me find a picture of an elephant."

"I need an alligator!" the boy with the chalky cheeks shouted.

Pips and I hurried around the room helping the kids find books and draw their animals.

"Miss Sadie." Charlotte waved me over to the bookshelf. "I can't find a book with tulips."

We flipped through book after book, and I found roses, violets, and daisies. Charlotte found lupines and lilies.

"Cici likes tulips," Charlotte insisted, her eyes bright. "And anyway, the flowers under her window are tulips, so that's what I'm going to draw."

She took my hand and led me back to her table. When she sat down, she took a scrap piece of paper and started sketching. After her first and second try, she tilted her head to look at her flowers.

"They should look softer," she finally said.

Smart girl. Her tulips were roughly the right shape, but she had trouble making the curves smooth.

"Maybe if you held your pencil a little more loosely," I suggested.

She tried again, and beamed up at me. "Yes!"

I'd worn that look before, many times, after Vivian had taught me some trick or other—pure happiness. I grinned and slid the fresh sheet of paper in front of her.

"I can't wait to see your field of tulips."

Three other kids were calling for me, so I hurried away to help. The class kept us so busy that I still hadn't drawn my elephant ears by the time the kids started finishing and waving their papers in the air, wanting Pips and me to come see.

Jess called out again, "Beetle!"

"Face," they all answered, made silly faces, and went dead silent again.

"Just nine more," Jess said. "Getting close now. When you're done with your drawings, bring them up to the carpet area. We'll share them all together."

It took about four minutes for the kids to settle in at the carpet area and put their papers on the floor in front of them. Most of their drawings had odd shapes and lumps, but I was astonished by their ideas. Charlotte had drawn a butterfly in her field of tulips, and said if she were a butterfly, she could sit outside her sister's hospital window. Jake, a boy who barely spoke through the entire lesson, said he'd be a lion so he could hang out with any animal in the forest. Isabel wouldn't share, but she had drawn herself as an alligator. I'd have to ask her about that sometime. Fritz refused to be an animal, and instead drew himself with a cape. He also insisted that I draw my elephant ears before they left for the day. I did, and then Jess lined the class up for their next activity.

"This will be so good for them," Jess said, as the kids followed another teacher out of the room.

"I wasn't sure they'd even understand the assignment," I said. "But they're amazing."

"People think six and seven year olds aren't deep thinkers, but that's because they don't take the time to really listen to kids." Jess said. "You girls did an excellent job today."

"Can we go wait in the parking lot for Grant?" I asked.

Jess rubbed her nose, looking uncomfortable. "I wish I could say yes, but I promised your mom I'd keep you inside until Grant came in for you."

I made a face. "He'll scare all the little kids."

"It will be okay," Pips said quickly. "We can just clean up in here and then prep for our next lesson while we wait."

Jess picked up her keys. "Okay. Thanks for everything, girls. I really am impressed."

As she left, I slumped into a chair.

"What's wrong, Sades? Didn't you think that went well?" Pips asked.

I didn't know where to start. "I don't want you missing out on everything because of me."

"Sadie, I'm the one who suggested coming to this camp. I want to be here. You're the one who wasn't sure about all the little kids, remember?"

What I really needed to talk about was Karl. But when I

opened my mouth to tell her, I stopped. Ruth and Andrew were already worried, and it wasn't really fair to make Pips worry too. I needed to 'fess up to Dad. No more stalling or putting it off. And I'd tell him about Charlotte, too.

"Have you heard from the girls?" I asked. "About Margo?"

"Bri called me last night and said she didn't have a plan yet. Margo hasn't cheated yet, or anything." Pips almost sounded disappointed.

"But that would be good, wouldn't it?" I asked. "If she didn't cheat, and Bri can win fair and square?"

"Yeah, I guess so," Pips didn't sound very sure. "Anyway, we're all getting together at Juliet's house tomorrow night to talk about it. You'll come, right?"

"Yeah, okay." Now I was the one who didn't sound sure. Maybe Margo would surprise them all, and the whole thing would just go away, and I would have one less problem to deal with. I could hope, at least.

"So what will we do tomorrow?" I asked.

Pips sat down with me. "I like Jess' idea about picture books."

"Oooh, yeah, me too." Now that I'd seen the kids in action, I could hardly wait to see what kinds of stories they'd write.

We started sketching out plans while we waited for Grant. After about fifteen minutes, he opened the classroom door, his face even blanker than usual.

"Let's go, girls."

"Is something wrong?" I asked.

"A film crew showed up outside, but they're distracted right now, so we need to go now."

I didn't like the sound of this. I put my notebook in my bag, and hurried down the hall behind Grant. "What, like a news reporter?"

"I think she's filming a documentary." Grant didn't offer any more information.

When we opened the church's front doors, a burst of noise met us. Three cameramen stood with bright lights aimed at a rumpled looking guy who had wrinkled clothes, mussed hair, and dark circles under his eyes, as though he hadn't slept for days. Jess stood behind him at the doors, her arm draped protectively across Charlotte's shoulders. A woman in tall heels held a microphone toward the guy she'd apparently trapped on the stairs.

"Do you have a statement, Mr. Walker?"

The man looked from one microphone to the other, and then back at Charlotte, who was wide-eyed, looking scared.

"I'll be happy to give you a statement in your studio, tomorrow. Right now, I need to take my daughter home." Mr. Walker, who must be Tyler, handed one of them his card, and then stepped away, scooping Charlotte up into his arms.

She buried her face in his neck as he brushed past the camera crews.

"Keep walking." Grant slipped behind Pips and me and didn't stop until we had climbed safely into the Hummer and closed the doors. He didn't turn the engine on right away. Instead, he watched the camera crew load up into their trucks, watching the parking lot.

"Who are you looking for?" I asked.

Grant ignored my question. "Did you know Tyler's daughter was in camp?"

Pippa and I exchanged a look.

"Yes." My voice sounded small.

Grant studied my face, his own expression impossible to read. "I promised to protect you, Sadie. I can't do that if you lie to me."

"She didn't lie," Pippa protested. "It was just—"

Grant's voice cut through Pippa's. "Do you understand me, Sadie?"

Pippa went still by my side while I picked miserably at my fingernails.

"Yes," I finally said.

"I'll fix this, then," Grant said.

"Actually, I need to talk to Dad," I said. "I'll tell you both everything tonight."

Grant eyed me in the mirror, but didn't press me to say more. In fact, no one said anything for the rest of the ride home.

Chapter 12

Secrets

My hand ached. I'd been drawing for hours. First, I'd drawn every single kind of door I could think of: a barn door, an old-fashioned ornate door, a modern steel door, a sliding glass door, a red door, a church door, a hospital door, a clubhouse door, a train door, a car door, a submarine door, a rickety old wooden door. When I'd started on an elevator door, I realized maybe this wasn't the best way to distract myself. So, I moved on to other kinds of escapes. Windows, hatches, trap-doors, secret panel doors. An escape. That was what I needed, and yet, I knew there was no way out. I'd have to tell the truth.

I turned to a fresh page and before I'd really thought it through, I realized I was drawing a close up of Karl's face, his eyes shadowy and deep. Maybe because I'd been thinking about doors all afternoon, I shaded the silhouette of a door into each of his eyes. I leaned back to look, and remembered someone, somewhere, saying something about eyes being windows to the soul. Well, maybe they could be a doorway, too. A way in or out. As far as I could tell, Karl needed out, out of whatever was inside him, torturing him.

I heard Dad pull into the driveway. Now or never. I walked downstairs and met him at the door. Higgins jumped up and tried to lick Dad's face, but I grabbed his collar.

"Down, Higgins," Dad said.

"Dad, I need to talk to you," I said, sick with fear.

Dad set down his briefcase. "I heard about the documentary crew. Tyler called me at the office. Imagine my surprise when I heard Charlotte's attending your camp."

"Dad, please just come in and sit down."

Grant and Mom were both on the couch already—they'd been watching the news. I switched off the television and faced them. Dad sat in his armchair.

I rubbed my sweaty palms on my jeans. Now that we were all here, I wasn't sure I could do this. My tongue felt too big for my mouth, and I had no idea where to start. The clock ticked. I hadn't realized how loud it was.

When I finally couldn't stand the silence anymore, I said, "I have to tell you something, but I need you to listen to everything before you say anything. Okay? Promise."

Dad made an impatient gesture, and pushed Higgins away. It really didn't help that Dad had already heard about the film crew. But I could have told him sooner. This all could have been so much easier.

I pressed on, clenching and unclenching my fists. "You know the day I came to your office and went to get cupcakes?"

Dad nodded, and I realized I didn't actually want to ask him questions. I wanted to just get this all out as quickly as I could.

"Well, that day, I got into the elevator to come back to your office, and Karl got in with me."

I ignored Mom's sharp intake of breath. "He told me about his sister, and asked me to convince you to take his side on things, and then he left the elevator. He didn't do anything bad ... "

When I looked around at all of their shocked expressions, I knew I still wasn't telling the entire truth. "But I was scared. Really scared. And I knew I should come right down and tell you. But you'd already given me all these rules, and I felt all cooped up and I didn't want you to worry, and I was pretty sure Karl would leave me alone after that."

No one said anything, and there was still more to tell. "I did know about Charlotte attending camp. Jess showed us some of the campers, and I knew. And today, when I saw her looking scared, watching her dad ... I don't know if it was my fault that those people showed up today. Maybe it was just a coincidence. But I didn't mean to do anything to hurt Charlotte, Dad, I really didn't. And I know I'm probably in tons of trouble, and everything, for keeping secrets, but please don't make me stop going to camp. Please? I didn't think I even wanted to be there, but then today I met all the kids and I just ... I want to be Charlotte's friend."

Dad took in a deep breath and blew it out. Then he crossed the room with unbelievable speed and pulled me into a tight hug.

When he finally let go, he held me by the shoulders and looked me straight in the eyes. "Sadie, if you ever, ever, keep a secret like that from me again, I don't know what I'll do. I love you. I'm trying to keep you safe. And if anything, especially my work, but anything at all, ever hurt you, I . . ."

Mom hugged me then, and they sat me down on the couch between them. Grant got up to leave, but Dad stopped him.

"We need to talk this through," Dad said. "Either Karl is following Sadie, and that was how he found Tyler and Charlotte, or he's following Charlotte or Tyler. In any case, the damage is done. Unless Tyler finds somewhere else to send Charlotte, Karl knows where Charlotte will be for the next few weeks. Tyler and Rebecca have their hands full with Cici at the hospital, so they have to send Charlotte somewhere. And if we station Grant outside the church, we can protect both girls at the same time."

Grant leaned up against the doorway, his hands in his pockets. "The camera crew was pushy, but they weren't working for a station. The woman said they were doing a documentary. And Tyler said he'd talk to them tomorrow in their studio."

Dad shook his head. "I don't know what to expect from either of them right now. Tyler's close to breaking because of Cici. And Karl just won't let up."

Mom gripped my hand, as though she thought I might suddenly disappear. Was Dad saying they'd let me keep teaching at camp?

"Sadie, you have to realize how serious this situation is," Dad said. "And you know there will have to be some kind of punishment for your lie. But I don't think banning you from camp is the right thing to do, for you or for Charlotte."

For the first time that night, I could breathe. He wasn't going to lock me in my room.

Dad walked over to the window and stared out at the darkening sky. "Normally, we'd ground you in a situation like this. But I'm not sure that's the right thing to do either. My work, and this totally out of your control situation, is partially to blame."

"Maybe instead of losing more privileges," Grant said, "Sadie could take on a responsibility instead?"

"That's what I'm thinking," Dad said. "I'll think about it. In the meantime, Sadie, I want you to promise me, absolutely promise, that no matter how small, you'll tell me any time you see Karl. Do you understand?"

I nodded, feeling like I might float up off the couch, feeling like poison had drained out of my body. Everything would be okay now.

Mom wrapped her arms around me. "Sadie, we love you so much."

"I love you, too, Mom." Her hair smelled like coconut shampoo.

"Stay for dinner, Grant?" Dad asked.

"Sure," Grant said.

Mom and Dad hurried off to the kitchen and Grant clapped a gigantic hand on my shoulder. "I'm proud of you, Sadie."

The weight of his hand reminded me of what he'd said about responsibility, and I didn't feel quite so floaty anymore. Not that I was worried about my punishment, really. But I suddenly realized how much I wanted Grant to stay proud of me. And now that I thought about it, telling my parents the truth only felt like the very first step.

"The girls are getting together tomorrow after camp," I told him. "To talk about Margo. And I still don't know what to do."

"Sleep on it," Grant said. "When the right moment comes, I think you'll know exactly what to say."

Hopefully, he was right.

Chapter 13

What Happens After You Die?

The kids wiggled excitedly on the carpet, their faces eager, as Pippa sat in the teacher chair. I loved watching Pips talk to the kids, loved watching them listen. I could have missed all this, but I was still here. I knew I was grinning like a crazy person.

"Who can tell me what a picture book is?" Pippa asked.

Hands shot up all across the room. Even Jake raised his hand. Pippa called on him.

"It's a book your mom or dad read to you before bed." Jake said. "With pictures."

A chorus of voices shouted out, adding to Jake's answer.

"I read picture books all day."

"I can read them by myself."

"My sister reads them to me."

"How many of you read picture books before bed?" Pippa asked, and just as they all opened their mouths to shout, she reminded them, "Raise your hands."

The air filled with raised hands.

Pippa pointed to me. "Sadie has some picture books you might recognize."

I held up *Where the Wild Things Are*, *Caps for Sale*, *Are You My Mother*, and *Knuffle Bunny*, and showed a few pages of each.

Pippa continued. "Picture books can have detailed pictures, or very simple pictures, but usually they combine words and pictures on each page. And picture books tell a story."

I joined Pippa at the front of the room as she continued, "We want you to pick a question that doesn't have an easy answer, like 'Why is the Sky Blue,' and write a story that answers the question. And for the next few days, we'll work on making it into a picture book."

"How many pages?" Fritz asked.

"As many as you want," I said. "We'll work on this project for the rest of the week, and on Friday, Jess will bind your books in her bookmaking machine so they look official."

"What kind of question?" Jake asked.

"Something hard to answer, like why do birds sing, or why do leopards have spots?" I answered.

"Or what happens after you die?" Charlotte asked.

I choked a little before I could answer, "Yes, or what happens after you die."

"What do you think happens?" Fritz asked.

My mouth went dry. Pips only shrugged, offering no help. Jess had left to prepare a snack, so I couldn't pass the question off to her.

"Me?"

"Yes, Miss Sadie, what do you think?" asked Fritz.

I cleared my throat. I knew the answer I was supposed to give, but it sounded too light with Charlotte watching my every move with her piercing blue eyes. She didn't want a vague, "You go to heaven." She wanted a real answer, one that helped her understand. I'd let her down yesterday, and I didn't want to do it again.

"It's a difficult question, Fritz," I finally said. "And I don't know exactly how it feels or what it looks like. No one does."

Charlotte didn't take her eyes off me, giving me no easy out. I glanced at Pippa again, but she watched me, waiting for an answer like everyone else. This wasn't the same as Jess asking me to be open if the kids asked about art and connecting with God. How had I been appointed the keeper of life's deepest truths? But as I remembered the conversation we'd had with Jess, I thought about my paintings, and I realized maybe I could answer, in my own way.

"I can't really picture heaven in my imagination," I said, finally. "But here's what I do know. Whenever I feel God come close to me, here, in my life on earth, the air becomes alive around me, the way it feels on a windy day when you can feel the air moving, but it isn't cold, it's warm with golden light. I think heaven will be like that, only better, because God will be near us all the time. Usually when God comes close to me, it's when I'm outside, or doing something I truly enjoy, like drawing, so that makes me think we won't just sit around in heaven. I think God will keep us busy doing the things we love. Other people have different ideas about heaven, and that's totally okay, too. We can't really know, not until we get there."

I stepped back, and thankfully, Pippa took the hint and switched back into teacher mode. "Why don't you turn to someone sitting close to you and tell them what you think heaven is like."

After they all shared their ideas, Pippa called, "Beetle!"

"Face," they all said.

The wacky faces never got old. Jess must have taught the kids this trick to make herself smile when the kids were spiraling out of control. It's hard to be upset when little kids make antennae fingers at you.

"So, remember," Pips said. "You can write your picture book about any question. If you want to write about heaven, you can, or you can write about any other hard-to-answer question."

The kids hurried back to their tables and started drawing right away. I circled the room. We had an excellent variety of stories starting. Fritz had titled his first page, "Why Superheroes Wear Capes," and had begun with a picture of a superhero in a dressing room trying on different clothes. Isabel had begun by drawing a rose.

"What are you going to write about, Isabel?" I asked, not really expecting an answer.

She still hadn't spoken in class.

She clamped her hand around my arm to pull me close, and whispered, "I'm writing about why roses grow in clumps instead of all by themselves."

Amazing.

After studying what she'd drawn so far, I said, "I love the texture on your rose petals. They look like alligator scales."

Her eyes lit up. "My favorite book is about an alligator. My mom used to read it to me."

She slipped back into silent mode, but I knew this tiny conversation was still a victory. Had she finally spoken to me because I'd braved telling the class what I really thought?

Charlotte smiled at me when I walked over to check on her.

"I didn't want to ask Cici about heaven," she said. "Because I don't want her to think too much about that. I want her to stay here with me."

Her words tugged at my heart, but I knew she didn't want sympathy. She wanted to speak her mind and be heard.

I took a closer look at her drawing, which showed a winged creature working at a blue workbench, shaping something with a small hammer. "So what are you drawing?"

"An ice city," Charlotte said. "I asked Cici why she thinks every snowflake is a different shape. And she said it's because there's a city of ice fairies who chip each one, and because they're artists, they never want to do the same thing twice."

"How does Cici tell you all these things?" I asked, truly wanting to know.

"She's not as far away as you think," Charlotte said, touching her heart. "She's right in here. Not like Jesus, different than that. But she's paying attention to what I do and she can tell me things."

I put a hand on her shoulder. "She's going to love your book, Charlotte. I can already tell."

Jess checked in now and again, but had to keep returning to the kitchen. Apparently her cake was prep-heavy. We let the kids draw until the end of the hour and sent them off to centers.

"Did you see Fritz's cape story?" Pippa asked. "After he goes to the Super-hero mall and tries on super hats and super shoes and super shorts, he decides he needs something even better. And that's when he finds a cape."

"I love it," I said. "I'm so glad we're doing picture books. And by the way, thanks for your help on the heaven question."

"What?" Pippa asked. "Your answer was amazing."

"What would you have said?" I asked.

"Probably something like you see a light and then go to heaven, where no one cries or gets hurt. That's what I've learned in Sunday school. But I liked your answer. And I liked that you told them you don't know. I don't think adults tell kids that very often."

"We're not adults, Pips."

"No, but we're ancient to these kids."

I laughed, feeling like a door had opened between us. Maybe it wouldn't be so hard for me to talk to Pips about God in person.

With a start, I remembered I hadn't told her yet. "Isabel talked to me, Pips."

Pippa's mouth dropped open. "No way."

"She told me she was writing about why roses grow in clumps."

"See? Good thing I didn't jump in and rescue you, then. Wow. Jess will be so amazed."

Grant opened the door and poked his head in. "Ready, girls? We're off to Juliet's house."

We followed him out to the Hummer, and this time the parking lot, fortunately, was camera-crew free.

Chapter 14

The Plan

Bri tossed a pillow at Juliet, missing her by miles. "No one wants tea sandwiches, Juliet. Starving. For Brownies!"

Juliet passed the pillow to Pippa. "You're the pitcher. Make sure you hit her in the nose. I made you a three-course snack, Bri. The least you can do is enjoy it."

Bri caught the pillow inches in front of her face. "Okay, okay. Tea sandwiches it is."

Juliet laid out a white tablecloth on the carpet and gave us each a white plastic plate, the fancy kind that looks like china until you pick it up. She had plastic champagne flutes, and she passed around sparking apple cider.

"I'll be right back with the first course," she said. "Cheers."

"Brownies!" Bri whined.

"Be nice, Bri," Alice said. "She worked hard."

Juliet brought back a three-tiered plate piled with tea sandwiches. She set it in the middle of the circle and pointed out the different flavors as she explained. "I made cucumber and cream cheese, rosemary chicken salad, peanut butter Doritos—in honor of Sadie and Pippa—pesto, brie, and tomato, and smoked gouda, turkey, and dill pickle. The dill pickles are for you, Bri."

"What's for me?" Alice asked, pretending to pout.

"The next course," Juliet said. "You'll see."

We dug in, and even Bri got over her brownie fixation as she crunched into the dill pickle sandwiches.

"We think we have a plan," Alice told Pippa and me.

Not what I wanted to hear.

"What?" Pips asked.

"Margo has no ideas. Her teammates never agree on anything. The only thing they've decided is to use black fabric and to ring their eyes with eyeliner so they look tough," Alice said.

"So, Margo will just lose on her own?" I asked hopefully.

"We don't have to count on it," Bri said. "Since Margo has already started snooping around, trying to swipe our designs, we'll just make it easy for her to cheat. Each designer has their own room where the other designers aren't supposed to go. While we work, we're totally isolated. If we leave the door unlocked, and maybe drop a few hints about being away for awhile, and rig up a video camera so we make sure to catch her, we've got her."

"You want her to cheat?" I asked.

"If she copies Bri's idea, probably the two of them will tie," Juliet said. "The other designer YaoYao is good, but she isn't as good as Bri. If Bri and Margo tie, we'll force Margo to forfeit the win and give it to Bri."

"Or else we'll show the video of her cheating," Alice added.

"So by tempting Margo to cheat, you're basically making sure Bri will win?"

"Perfect, isn't it?" Juliet asked.

I exchanged a look with Pippa, who now picked at her sandwich nervously. Didn't they realize they were planning to cheat in order to catch a cheater? Pips knew. I could see the worry clearly on her face. Maybe she'd thought more about what I'd said about blackmail after all.

"Maybe we should just let Margo lose on her own, like Sadie said," Pippa finally said.

"You can't just wait for everything to work out on its own," Alice said. "Sometimes you have to take things into your own hands."

"I'm just not sure cheating is the right—"

Alice made an exasperated sound. "What? I suppose you two think we should just pray about it?"

Pips flinched at the sarcasm in Alice's voice. Grant was wrong. The moment had come and I had absolutely no idea what to say. The silence crackled with tension.

Finally, Pips sighed. "What do you want Sadie and me to do?"

Bri clapped her hands and made a little squeal of happiness. "I knew you'd come through. Come to the show.

Snap some photos. Document the moment of misery for Margo, and maybe we'll send her an album. You know, so she doesn't forget that cheating doesn't pay."

The matching triumphant expressions on my friends' faces made the tea sandwiches gurgle in my stomach. I couldn't look at Pips, not now.

"I'll be back," I said, hurrying out of the room and down the stairs.

As I headed for the back door, wanting some air, I passed the living room where Grant sat, watching something on his iPad. I heard a familiar voice.

"The device tests for a genetic strain of cancer," the man said.

I moved closer to see if it really was Tyler on screen.

Grant glanced up, saw me, and motioned to the space on the couch next to him. "Tyler gave the interview, and your Dad passed the footage on to me ... "

The reporter who'd grilled Tyler on the church steps steepled her fingers. "You're working with a mediator in order to secure your patent, is that right?"

Tyler sat straight and still, his expression mild. "Yes. Karl and I have a difference of opinion on how the device, which is now in preliminary stages, should be tailored. He feels we should test adults, to prescreen for the possibility of the gene in their children. In his opinion, when a mother and father have a high likelihood of passing on the gene, families should adopt or not have children at all instead of subjecting a child to the possibility of this cancer. I had always planned to test children. Studies have begun to show that proactive use of hormones at an early age can effectively 'shut off' the gene, stopping the cancer."

I leaned forward, my interest peaked, as the reporter asked the question I wanted to know. "Why don't doctors treat all children with the potential gene?"

"Cost, mostly," Tyler answered. "And the hormones aren't harmless. Like any other treatment, complications are possible."

The reporter frowned. "And why can't the device do both? Test both adults and children? Leave it up to the individual and their doctor how they want to proceed?"

"Exactly!" I felt like shouting. Tyler didn't miss a beat. "As in all medical research, there are limits of time and money. The simpler test is whether a child has the gene. If we tailor the device in this way, it could be ready to use next year. Testing two adults and understanding the probability of the gene showing up in their children is more difficult, and would take a much longer process to get right. Starting with the simpler test is more scientifically sound."

"And quicker," the reporter said. "I'm sure you'd like the device ready as soon as possible. Is it true that you have twin girls, one with this very cancer and one without?"

Tyler held the reporter's eyes. "Yes."

"So this test could save your daughter's life, isn't that right?"

"Yes," Tyler said.

No. Please God, don't let Charlotte get sick.

Somehow I hadn't put together the fact that Cici's cancer was genetic, and that as her twin, Charlotte, would be at high risk, too. I'd been too focused on Charlotte's sadness about her sister. My queasiness was back. I hurried out to the back steps, put my head between my knees and breathed deep.

A few minutes later, Grant came out to join me.

"Okay?" he asked.

I managed a weak smile. "Too many tea sandwiches."

"I hear the girls have already finished course two — sushi — and are on to the brownies. Are they really as good as everyone says?"

"Delicious. But I couldn't eat one now to save my life."

"After you left, Tyler told the reporter that he's pausing the mediation process until Cici is finished with her treatment. It sounds like there have been complications."

I hugged my knees to my chest. "But she'll be all right, won't she?"

Grant stared at his shoes. "I don't know, Sadie."

No one I'd known had ever had cancer, and even though I didn't actually know Cici, I felt like I did. And knowing that Charlotte could get sick too made me want to run and scream and smash fragile things on the ground. I almost wished Karl would show up again, so I could do a little shouting myself. How could he keep Tyler from finishing the device, just because he was afraid that kids would be born with the cancer gene?

This test could save Charlotte's life. If Karl had his way,

kids like Charlotte and Cici, kids who might possibly get sick, would never have the chance to be born at all. The thought made me cold and empty. Sickness was horrible, especially in someone you loved. After watching Mom collapse many times, I knew, firsthand. Still, would it be better to not have the chance to love someone just because they might eventually die and leave you? The argument didn't make sense.

"Can we go home?" I asked Grant.

"Sure, if you're ready," Grant said.

"I should go say goodbye to the girls." I pushed past the coldness, an echo of the hollowed-out feeling I'd battled all spring, and went upstairs to Juliet's room.

"You missed the sushi, Sades," Juliet said.

"I'm sorry, Juliet." I couldn't meet anyone's eyes. "I'm not feeling well and Grant is taking me home. But I'll be there on Friday for your show, Bri, okay?"

"You have to get better," Bri said. "Saturday's waterskiing."

I nodded, and forced a smile.

"Call me if you're still sick in the morning," Pips said.

The girls gave me sympathetic waves as I closed the door. Off to home, to my sketchbook, to my soft, soft bed. Maybe I could close my eyes and just forget everything for a while.

From: Sadie Douglas
To: Frankie Paulson
Date: Tuesday, June 14, 8:22 pm
Subject: RE: Creaky old gate

Hey! I was thinking of painting a creaky old gate, but I haven't found one yet. I liked your collage. What did you use? Tin foil? I hope someday I can see your collages in person, because I know they must be even more amazing when you can see them in three-dimension. I like your idea to carve out some of the pages to make room for the collages to keep the book from getting too thick.

I also liked Vivian's sequence of three drawings, showing the puddle as a door into a watery world. I'm going to try something like that.

Okay. I need to tell you something, and sorry for the total mood switch. I'm helping at a camp. I think I told you. And there's this girl, Charlotte, and her sister has cancer. And it sounds like the cancer is getting bad. I'm afraid to go to camp tomorrow, because Charlotte is always asking me impossible questions, and I don't know how to answer her if she asks me if her sister might die.

What do you think I should do?

From: Sadie Douglas
To: Frankie Paulson
Date: Tuesday, June 14, 9:10 pm
Subject: RE: Creaky old gate

Thanks, Frankie. That's good advice. You're right. I should be there for her, even if I can't answer her questions. I promise to draw a door sometime soon, when things settle down around here.

Chapter 15

Chinese Jump Rope

We'd only talked with the class for a minute at camp that morning, and then sent the kids off to continue working on their books. Today, the kids would finish their rough draft art in pencil and tomorrow we'd bring out watercolors, colored pencils, and pastels. Every other minute someone called us over, asking how to spell monkey or girl or cloud or once upon a time.

Pippa came up behind me. "How are you feeling today, Sadie? Better?"

"Yeah." Pips must have been miserable yesterday, probably thinking I'd left because of the Margo-plan, and because she'd given in to the girls. And I wasn't happy about that, not at all, but I hadn't exactly stood up to them either, in the end. I wanted to explain about Tyler's interview, that I was also worried about Charlotte, and Cici ... I was seriously a disaster magnet.

Jess, who was cutting out bulletin board shapes at the back of the room, held up her buzzing phone and mouthed, "I need to get this."

She went out into the hall to talk for a few minutes and then came back in, much more pale than she'd been when she left.

"Girls?" She motioned Pips and me over.

We gathered close.

"It's Cici," Jess said. "Her fever spiked this morning and the doctors think she may have caught some kind of infection. With little to no white blood cells, this is highly dangerous. Tyler and Rebecca need to stay with her in the hospital overnight, but they don't want Charlotte to worry. They asked if I could help them find somewhere fun for Charlotte to spend the night."

"She can come to my house," I said, knowing my parents would be all right with this. "I've shown her a picture of Higgins and she said she wanted to meet him."

"Would you really do that, Sadie?" Jess asked. "Charlotte loves you and I know she'd love to spend the evening with you."

"I'd come, but I have a soccer pick up game tonight," Pips said. "Every Wednesday to keep us in shape over the summer."

Of course, Charlotte and I could draw or paint, but she'd done a bunch of that already today. We could play with

Higgins as long as we stayed inside. What had I liked to do when I was six? And then I had the perfect idea.

"Let me call Grant and ask him to check with my parents," I said.

I borrowed Jess' phone to call, and then she called Tyler and Rebecca to ask them about the plan. Everyone agreed that we should wait to tell Charlotte until after camp.

"She'll be excited, but also afraid for Cici," Jess said after she got off the phone. "I'd rather she finish the day without having to worry."

Grant picked us up after class and brought Pips home. Afterward, we went to the toy store so I could pick up a surprise for Charlotte, and then we dropped by her house to pack her a bag and grab a booster seat for the Hummer. At the end of the camp day, Grant pulled into the church parking lot, and we went in to find Charlotte

After I told her about the sleepover, she looked up at me with those intense eyes. "It's because Cici is really sick, isn't it?"

I couldn't lie to her. "Yes, she's having trouble today."

Charlotte bit her lip and nodded. "I asked her a couple questions this morning, and she didn't answer. I was pretty sure something was wrong."

"Your parents will stay overnight at the hospital and do everything they can for Cici, and we're going to try to have some fun, you and I," I said. "You get to meet Higgins, and we can paint, if you want, and I have a surprise for you too."

Grant let Charlotte play with all the buttons in the Hummer before we took off. We stopped for ice cream, and then again at one of the horse farms, and one of the horse trainers let Charlotte feed carrots to the horses. When we finally got home, I stopped before opening the front door.

"Now, Higgins will charge at you and put his paws up on your shoulders and lick your face, because he wants to show you how much he loves you. Do you want me to catch him first?"

Charlotte shook her head. "No. I don't mind getting licked."

Sure enough, Higgins barreled down the stairs the minute we opened the door. I stood behind Charlotte so she wouldn't topple over when Higgins jumped up on her, but he surprised me by being mostly gentle. He ran right over, but then stopped and did the full-body wag thing, his tongue hanging out.

Charlotte held out her hand and Higgins sniffed it, and then used his nose to flip her hand up on top of his head.

"He wants you to scratch his ears," I said.

She did, and he sat down, his rope-like tail thumping on the wood floor.

"So, are you ready for your surprise?" I asked.

Charlotte grinned, and I showed her up to my room. Just for fun, I'd had the toy-store wrap the gift, because everyone liked unwrapping boxes, even if the presents were little. Charlotte ripped off the paper and then held out the long thin band to me, a question on her face.

"It's a Chinese jump rope. Here, look."

After looping the band around the back legs of my desk

chair, I piled books on the seat, weighing it down. Then, I showed Charlotte where to stand, and helped her loop the band around her legs too. I stood in the middle and demonstrated the jumping pattern.

"Ten, Twenty, Thirty, Forty," I said, jumping so first the left side of the rope was between my feet, and then the right, and doing that again. "Out, in, step, in, on." The end of the pattern was both feet outside the band, both in, slowly stepping on both sides, the first time I'd allowed my feet to touch the bands, then in again, and then jumping so I landed one foot on one side of the band, and the other foot on the other side.

"Can I try?" Charlotte asked.

I traded her places, and she jumped while I helped her count. Once she figured out the basic pattern, I showed her some of the more complicated levels, like diamonds. Mom came upstairs to cheer us on when we got to our championship level. We jumped until we were both exhausted.

Dad made macaroni and cheese with chicken for dinner, and while we ate, Charlotte's eyes began to close. Perfect. The evening had worn her out, and now she could sleep.

Please, let Cici be all right. Let Charlotte wake up tomorrow to good news about her sister.

Dad carried Charlotte up to my room, and I helped her find her pajamas and brush her teeth. Mom had inflated the air mattress for me to sleep on, and changed the sheets on my bed so Charlotte could sleep there.

I wasn't quite ready to sleep, but I knew if I took out my

sketchbook now, before Charlotte had fallen asleep, I'd keep her awake. So, after I tucked the covers around Charlotte, I headed toward the air mattress.

"You aren't going to read me a story?" Charlotte asked, her voice slow and sleepy.

"I don't have any, I don't think," I said.

"Tell me a story, then," Charlotte said. "About one of those times, like you said at camp, where you knew God was there."

Now what? When I'd said that at camp, I'd been talking about my paintings. Now looking at them, I had another inspiration. Still, my hands shook a little as I took the painting of Higgins and me in the church off the wall. I'd only told this story to a few people. But of all people, I was pretty sure Charlotte would understand.

"It's not a picture book, but it's a picture at least," I said.

"Did you paint that?" Charlotte asked.

"Yes." I told her the story of how I'd ended up in a church last fall, in the snow, by myself with Higgins, how I'd felt so alone and afraid and hadn't known what to do and then suddenly, I'd known I wasn't alone.

"I'm going to try to tell Cici that story," Charlotte said. "Maybe she even knows what that feels like. I hope so."

"I hope so too, Charlotte."

"Can Higgins sleep on the bed with me?" she asked.

"I'll call him up and see if he stays. Sometimes he gets too hot," I said.

Charlotte's eyes began to close again. Higgins circled a few times and then curled up at her feet.

"Night, Charlotte."

"Night, Sadie."

Please, give her sweet dreams.

I took out my sketchbook, and sat on the air mattress, drawing her small face, her expression serious, even in sleep.

And protect her from all bad things: sickness and sadness and pain.

I closed my sketchbook and looked out at the stars, which usually made me feel so safe and comforted. Tonight, I didn't want to think about heaven or anything beyond this small room. Like Charlotte, I wanted to think about the here and now, and keep the people I loved close. I lay down, and played with my star earring, thinking of all the people I loved who were so far beyond my reach. The empty, lonely feeling grew so large I felt like I might disappear inside myself.

You are not alone.

The thought, warm and calming, wrapped around me, reminding me yet again that I didn't have to do this on my own, no matter how many times I forgot.

Thank you.

From: Sadie Douglas
To: Ruth Manning
Date: Thursday, June 16, 6:55 pm
Subject: Tomorrow

Tomorrow the kids are putting together their picture books, and then in the evening, Pips and I are going to the fashion show. The girls caught Margo on camera stealing their designs, so tomorrow night they are going to tell her that if she wins or ties, she will have to forfeit on her own or they will show the video of her cheating. The thing is, this basically guarantees that Bri's team will win, which feels a lot like cheating to me. Pips agrees with me, I know, but we still haven't talked about it. So now, we're supposed to go to the fashion show and take pictures of the whole thing. I keep hoping I'll come up with some brilliant way to get out of this. But so far, I've got absolutely zero ideas.

Charlotte's sister, Cici, was really sick yesterday, but they were able to use antibiotics and her fever came down. If you think about her, please pray.

Sounds like the twins have been crazy. I'm glad you're still earning money to come out here at the end of the summer, though. I can't wait!

Chapter 16

Forfeit

Pips and I maneuvered down a row around the middle of the auditorium, and found two empty seats near the middle of the room. Grant had opted to sit in the back, but I still squirmed in my seat, knowing he was nearby. After everything happened tonight, he'd know I hadn't stood up to the girls. I could still feel his hand on my shoulder, hear him saying, "I'm proud of you, Sadie." Not after tonight, he wouldn't be. I sighed as we flipped open our programs.

Pips pointed to the names. "Margot's second and Bri is third."

"Maybe they won't tie," I suggested hopefully, reading the other name. "Maybe this other girl, YaoYao, will win?"

"Alice was pretty sure that wouldn't happen." Pips took out her camera and checked the flash and settings.

"They were going to show the video to Margo right before the competition?" I asked.

Pips nodded miserably. "Sadie, I know I should have done something to stop them, but Alice . . ."

The lights went down and the music started.

The judges were in the front row, three rows ahead of us. The runway stretched out into the audience, and a spotlight flashed on, highlighting YaoYao's first model. She wore a fancy dress covered in silver sequins, with a rose pattern in red sequins on the skirt. YaoYao obviously liked sequins, because the next model wore a sequin-covered skirt and top, but this time the rose was yellow, and on the shirt. The third model wore jeans and a t-shirt, and the jeans were covered with a vine of pink roses, in sequins, of course.

YaoYao stepped out from the curtain after the three girls had modeled, wearing purple sequins and a rose of her own on her otherwise black pants and black stretchy tee.

"What does the rose symbolize?" One of the judges asked.

"To me, a rose is the perfect flower," YaoYao said, and beamed around at the crowd. "A red rose might mean love, but a yellow rose can mean friendship. The roses on each of my designs are meant to make the person wearing them and the people around them feel very particular feelings."

"But not everyone knows what each color of rose means," Pippa whispered to me.

The audience applauded loudly as YaoYao left the stage.

"The judges seemed to like the symbolism, though.

140

Maybe she'll win," I whispered back as Margo's first model took the stage.

Pips gave me a worried look. "I don't want Bri to lose, though."

"I just don't want her to win by cheating, Pips."

Pips bit her lip. "I know."

Margo's designs combined very different kinds of textures, like floaty see-through fabric over velvet, or what looked like fishnet over jeans. She used all black in each design, and the models' makeup was thick, especially around their eyes.

Margo explained to the judge that she used mostly black because she felt that clothes were part of the way you showed the world you were powerful and strong. And black was a strong, powerful color. Margo looked directly at Pippa, then, and raised a challenging eyebrow.

"What did that mean?" I asked.

But Juliet had already come out on stage. Bri had designed a dress for her that was both totally Bri, and perfect for Juliet. The knee-length skirt was made of a silky purple fabric, with that fish-net fabric in lavender over the top. She wore a sheer hot-pink shirt with a lace-up vest over the top made from this cool patterned velvet that was mostly purple, aqua and hot pink. Juliet also wore hot pink tights with purple polka dots and aqua boots that came to mid-calf. It was a wild outfit, but because the colors were so spot on, and because Juliet had all that flowing blond hair to set it off, it was perfect.

Alice came out next in jeans and a t-shirt. But Bri had first dyed the jeans bright green, and then added iron-on velvety designs in lime green and bright blue. Bri had added bright blue lace to a light blue t-shirt, and torn off the sleeves, adding green see-through fingerless gloves to the mix. Alice wore her usual Chuck Taylors, but with green laces to match the gloves, and her long dark hair hung free down her back.

Bri didn't have another model, so she had to wear her final outfit, black and white striped leggings, with a sleeveless top that was half-dress, half-shirt with a funky, uneven hem. The fabric was a patchwork of many different textures of fabric: lace, silk, and that fish-net stuff, all sewed on top of a deep red velvet. She wore fuzzy red boots and her hair up in a bun with two black and red hair-sticks sticking out.

After Bri had finished walking the runway, the judges asked her about the colors she'd chosen.

"Color is one way that people express their personality," Bri said. "And lots of people are afraid to wear color, but they shouldn't be. People just need to find the right colors for themselves."

Pips and I stood and clapped as the girls left the stage. The judges conferred for a moment, and then the woman went to the microphone. The crowd hushed, waiting for the announcement.

"We've decided to do an unprecedented thing this year," the woman judge announced. "Will Brianna Ingles and Margo Martin please join us on stage?"

No. Couldn't they just decide that YaoYao should win? I

exchanged uncomfortable looks with Pips as Bri and Margo re-entered the stage, their models trailing after them.

"You girls had very similar concepts, but handled them with different color schemes," the judge said. "We can't decide between the originality and uniqueness of your designs, and so we are going to award you both first place prizes. You and your teams are both invited to come work with our designers next week, and we will simply split the time. Congratulations on your excellent work."

No one had accused anyone of cheating. I watched Margo as the judge climbed the stairs, reaching out to shake her hand. Margo's face twisted with anger and frustration as she glared first over at Bri, Juliet and Alice, and then out at Pippa and me.

"Would you like to say anything?" the judge asked Margo.

"I ..." Margo began, and then cleared her throat. "I'm sorry, I can't accept this award."

Anger and embarrassment battled on her face.

"Pippa, we can't just sit here," I hissed.

"But what are we supposed to do?" She stared down at the camera miserably.

I grabbed her arm "No, Pips. No pictures."

"Alice will kill me," Pips whispered.

"Bri cheated and won," I said. "Isn't that bad enough?"

"I just ... I ... " Confusion crossed Pippa's face, but she gave the girls on stage one last look, and then turned off the camera.

I didn't mean to ask Pips to choose between me and the other girls. And I knew she still felt unsure about what the right thing was to do. She'd been so sure when she'd explained the club to me, confident that putting bullies in their place was right. I hadn't exactly helped by just running away from the problem a few days ago. Eventually, I'd have to tell the girls what I really thought.

Onstage, Bri, Alice, and Juliet sparkled with happiness. Like instead of just humiliating someone, they had just scored a huge victory.

The judge blinked at Margo, as though she hadn't quite understood what she'd said. "I'm sorry, did you say you cannot accept this award?"

"Yes, that's what I said," Margo snapped. She turned on her heel, and her models followed her, clearly arguing with her all the way off stage.

After trying to cover the awkward moment with an overdone laugh, the judge walked over to Bri. "I don't suppose you have any difficulty accepting this award?"

Bri beamed out at the crowd. "No, and I'd like to thank the judges for this amazing opportunity."

She gave big hugs to Alice and Juliet and then the three of them grabbed hands and bowed, before they bounded offstage. Pippa's shoulders drooped as we found our way out of the theatre and looked for the girls. I made a point of not catching Grant's eye. Sure, we hadn't taken any pictures. But we hadn't stopped the humiliation either.

"Wasn't that amazing?" Juliet asked, pulling Pips into a huge hug. "Did you see her face?"

Bri grabbed me and squeezed me tight. "And her models didn't even know. We wouldn't let her tell anyone."

"Did you get the pictures?" Alice asked Pippa.

"Oh, yeah, the pictures. You took one of her face when she turned down the award, right?" Bri asked.

"No," I said.

Bri's face fell. "What happened, Pips?"

"She just looked so miserable," Pips ventured. "I didn't want to take a picture of that."

Alice gave Pips a puzzled look. "But that was the whole point. She was supposed to be miserable, and the pictures would have made sure she never forgot."

Pips stared at her shoes. Now really wasn't the best time for this conversation. Maybe we could talk about it tomorrow at the lake. A lot of this was my fault, and I shouldn't let Pips take the blame.

I looked around to see if Grant had followed us out of the theater. As I scanned the room, I saw him leaning against the railing that led up to the theatre. I couldn't see the disappointment on his face, but I still knew it was there.

"We should probably go, Pips." I tried to smile at the other girls. "Don't forget, tomorrow's waterskiing. Dad's starting the pick up run at seven am, so no sleeping in."

"I don't think I'll ever sleep again after this," Bri said.

I backed away with Pips, while Alice, Bri, and Juliet kept hugging one another. They grinned and told each other how amazing that had been and rehashed the look on Margo's face as she turned down the award. It was like watching someone else's friends.

We picked our way across the crowd to Grant, and the closer we came, the worse I felt. Grant wouldn't be around much longer, now that Tyler had decided to call off the mediation for a while. Tonight, Dad had said that maybe even as soon as next week, I might not need a bodyguard anymore. While on the one hand, everything returning to normal was a huge relief, I didn't want Grant to leave disappointed in me.

Pips kept looking back at the others, who were huddled tightly, laughing every now and then. If it came down to choosing between them and me, what would she do? What if I had changed so much or the others had changed so much, that we couldn't bridge the gap? The aching loneliness opened up inside me again, and I wished I could curl up on the floor, right here, and hold myself together. Or have someone else wrap me up in their arms and make me feel like I wasn't made of air and feathers, but like something solid.

"Ready to go, girls?" Grant asked.

I hugged my arms tight and nodded.

Chapter 17

Ambush

"Hit it!" I called, and Dad gunned the boat.

I kept my knees bent and pulled with my arms, but right after I popped up out of the water, I face-planted back down. As I bobbed back up to the surface, the boat circled around. The girls' happy voices rang out over the lake. Somehow, today, it felt like last night hadn't existed. We'd packed into Dad's Jeep and driven up here, and Grant hadn't even had to come, because Mom and Dad were with us. Finally, it felt like a regular summer Saturday, as we piled into the motorboat and took turns waterskiing. I knew I'd have to talk to the girls eventually. But right now, I wanted to hold on to this happy, back-with-the-girls feeling.

"You okay, Sadie?" Juliet called.

"She's fine." Pips laughed. "She has to crash and burn a

few times every time we go out before she remembers how to do it."

"Ha, ha!" I grabbed the rope and prepped myself again.

She was right. As a general rule, I had two crashes for every good run. But this time, I was going to get up on top of the water.

I breathed in the cold Tahoe air, and shook out my shoulders. Relax, Sadie. Keep your knees bent. See yourself on top of the water. Don't think. It's just you and the water.

"Hit it," I called.

Again, the boat's motor gunned, and I pulled back hard, keeping my knees bent. I was plowing through the water, not quite up, and not quite down.

"Stand up NOW," Pips called.

I pushed up and rebalanced, and suddenly, I was skimming across the lake. Since it was afternoon, the water was pretty choppy, but I managed to hold on. The girls cheered from the boat and a goofy grin spread across my face. Dad turned in a wide loop and I arced out across the water. If Pips were skiing, she'd be crossing over and across the wake, but I was happy right here, behind the boat, letting the boat and the water take me where it chose.

Finally, my arms and legs began to shake from holding tight for so long. I threw up my arms and sunk down into the water.

The boat circled around and I climbed back in, wrapping myself in the towel Pips offered.

"I say we cook hot dogs and marshmallows over a campfire before we drive home," Dad said. "What do you girls think?"

"Ooooh!" Juliet clapped her hands. "Are we going to a store? I can do gourmet s'mores."

Bri elbowed her. "But regular hot dogs, right? Because I like mine burnt and crispy."

"We can get fancy barbecue sauce or mustard or something," Juliet said.

"All right," Dad said. "We'll find a campsite and Cindy and whoever wants to stay can work on gathering wood for the fire and roasting sticks, and the rest of us can go to the store."

"Why don't Sadie and I stay," Pips said.

"Sounds good." Dad maneuvered the boat to shore and we carried our gear up to the Jeep. We always put in the boat near a campground where Dad knew the owners, and they generally let him use a site for the afternoon, even if he wasn't planning to spend the night. We found an empty spot, and waved the others off. Mom had brought her recliner chair and a book, so she settled in, and Pippa and I headed into the trees to find kindling. I found a spot under a tree where some branches had fallen and started gathering sticks.

"Pips, about Margo . . ."

"What about her?" Pippa crouched down to gather sticks of her own. "I mean, it's all over, isn't it?

"But it was wrong, Pips, you know it was."

Pippa dropped her sticks on the ground and sat on a log. "Margo has been bullying people all year, Sades. No, it wasn't right, but maybe Margo will lay off now. Maybe we can all just let it go."

"But what about the next time the girls want to gang up on someone?" I came over to sit next to Pippa.

She kicked at the dirt. "I don't know, Sadie. Before you and I talked, I thought what we were doing was right. And I'm still not sure it isn't. And Alice thinks ..."

"What?" I asked.

"That it's because I'm Christian that I'm questioning the club," Pippa picked up her sticks and walked away from me.

I followed her, trying to get her to look at me. "When did she say that?"

"Alice was really upset after you left Juliet's house. She thinks you're making me choose between you and the others, that this bullying thing is just the beginning. And she thinks I don't want to be her friend because she's an aetheist."

"But that's not true—"

Pippa's look cut into me, and I remembered my thoughts last night, watching the girls, walking away with Pips. She turned away from me and knelt down for more sticks.

I knelt down next to her. "Pips, I'd never want you to choose between me and the girls. You know that."

"Everything has been so strange between me and Alice, even with the other girls, ever since you got back," Pippa said.

It was like everything I'd worried about, from the first minute when Pips had shown me the pictures on her iPhone, it was all coming true. And I didn't know what to do to stop it.

"Pips, I ..."

"Look, I just need, I don't know, Sades. I need time to think, to figure this all out. I want you to be happy and I want Alice to be happy, and I don't know what to do." Her eyes welled with tears.

Something between us was breaking, slipping apart, something neither of us could fix. More than anything, I wanted to smooth things over, make everything right between us again, but I didn't know what to say.

She turned away from me. "My arms are full. Let's take these back to the campsite and then we can come back for more."

We piled our kindling by the fire pit. Without discussing it, I went one direction for more, and Pippa went the other. Never, never ever, in our lives, had there been trouble between us that I couldn't fix.

I found some long sticks and stripped off the extra branches, making them into roasting sticks. I also found a few logs left behind by campers, and carried those back to the fire pit. Dad would probably need to buy a bundle of wood from the campsite manager too, but the logs would be a good start. Maybe I could find some more kindling down by the lake. I walked in the direction of the loading dock, realizing I was alone for the first time since Dad had hired Grant.

The hairs on the back of my neck stood up, and I tried to tell myself I was just imagining things, but I had the creepy feeling someone was watching me. I turned a full circle, scanning the trees, but didn't see anything. I was fine. Karl hadn't shown up ever, since the elevator, and why would he be all the way out here, in Tahoe, anyway? Especially now that Tyler had dropped the case?

I found a new patch of kindling and started filling my arms.

"Hello, Sadie."

I whirled around. It wasn't possible. It was almost as though because I'd imagined him, now here he was in real life.

I backed away. "What are you doing here?"

"I don't think you spoke to your dad," Karl said. "Or at least you didn't convince him. And now, Tyler's dropping the case. Just when it was about to end up in court."

I stumbled over a root as I continued to back up, but I managed not to fall.

"You promised to talk to your dad for me, Sadie." Karl kept forcing me toward the water.

"You know how important this is. I explained it to you."

Like Mom said, it was the missing logic that made Karl so frightening. Why would he follow my family all the way to Tahoe, wait until I was alone, corner me on the beach? What possible reason could he have to do this? I'd thought that the next time I saw Karl, I would shout at him, tell him how wrong he was about the device, about Tyler. I'd tell him about Charlotte. But I couldn't bring myself to say anything at all.

Just as my feet splashed into the water, Dad burst from the trees. He stopped to take in the situation, me in the lake,

Karl, still moving toward me. I'd never seen Dad run so fast. He plowed into Karl and knocked him to the sand.

"What are you doing?" he demanded, standing over Karl with fists clenched. "What are you doing?"

Even on the ground, Karl radiated with intensity. "I told you, Matthew, that I would have my way. So Tyler wants a break from the case. Too bad. It's time that this was decided. And I thought Sadie could help me ..."

"Help you what?" Dad looked like he might punch Karl any minute.

"Explain things to you," Karl said, standing, brushing sand off his jeans. "But, I can see you won't be reasonable. I don't know why I expected you to be."

Even now, Karl wasn't backing down. Dad took out his phone.

"Call the police," Karl said, holding up his hands. "Tell them I talked to your daughter. It's not a crime. The next time I see you will be in court, anyway."

Karl turned to go, and as soon as he was a few steps away, Dad scooped me up out of the water and held me tight. I couldn't stop shaking.

"Let's get you back to the campfire," Dad said, and guided me toward the trees.

Mom ran up then, and seeing the look on Dad's face and my soaked shoes, she said, "What happened, Matthew?"

When she pulled me into a hug, Dad made a horrible, angry growl. "Karl showed up. He just won't stop."

"Matthew ..." Mom warned.

Dad ran his fingers though his hair. "I'm sorry, Cindy. I'm sorry, Sadie. I just feel so helpless. I think we should get Sadie out of here."

"You mean you want to go home before the campfire?" Mom asked.

"No, we should eat or the girls will be starving on the way home. But tomorrow, we're finding a way to send Sadie out of town. Could she go stay with your sister?"

Mom bit her lip. "I'm not sure. I don't think I can travel anywhere right now."

"I know you're not up to it just now, but we can send Sadie," Dad said.

"You're sending me on a trip, by myself?" I asked.

"You'll be safe anywhere but here," Dad said. "I just want you to go for a few weeks until we can get this thing into court and legally tie Karl's hands so he can't keep harassing you."

"What if ..." Mom began. "What if we sent Sadie to Owl Creek?"

I stared at her, not daring to believe she had just suggested Owl Creek.

I twisted my earring around nervously before asking, "Could I go visit ... Vivian?"

Probably best not to ask about Andrew just now.

Mom looked relieved, as though she'd thought she'd have to sell me on this more. "Yes. Owl Creek would be perfect, Matthew, don't you think? We know Sadie's safe there, and she's comfortable there."

"I'll think about it," Dad said, and then seeing the expression on my face, he added, "But don't get too excited, Sadie. I haven't decided yet, all right?"

I tried to rearrange my face into a less hopeful expression.

"All right. Let's go get this fire started," Dad said.

Vivian. Ruth. Frankie. And Andrew. I nearly floated over to join the girls.

Chapter 18

Miles

Mom and Dad had special passes to help me through security, and once we arrived at the gate, they started fussing over me all over again.

"Are you sure she should go on her own?" Mom asked Dad. "What if Karl or ... "

"Karl's focus is entirely on the case," Dad said. "And when Tyler and I spoke last night, he agreed to go to court. He wanted to wait, but Cici's condition is so up and down, the doctors aren't sure whether she'll be in limbo for weeks or months. And every day they wait to start work on the device is another day Charlotte has to wait for her own test. Plus, we both agree that something has to be done about Karl."

"I can't imagine how Tyler must feel," Mom said. "I wish we could do something for him."

Neither Dad nor I answered. We both wished we could do something too. The trouble was, no one knew what that was.

Please, God, let Cici pull through. And keep the cancer far from Charlotte.

"Are you hungry, Sadie?" Mom asked. "We could buy you some snacks, or a soda?"

"I'm fine, Mom."

If it wasn't for Charlotte and Cici, I'd be better than fine. This morning had been a whirlwind of packing and Dad on the phone making plans with Ruth's family to pick me up at the airport. I'd stay with them, since Vivian was living in her trailer now and had very little extra room. After Dad had made sure I'd have somewhere to stay, he found airline tickets and figured out all the rules of a minor traveling by herself. I'd never traveled without my parents, so while they were totally worried, I could hardly stand still because of all the shivery excitement surging through me. And to top everything off, my parents had given me a phone—an old flip phone, but who cared—so that I could call if I needed anything. I'd promised only to use the phone for emergencies. But still!

When I got off the plane, Ruth's dad would meet me at the gate, since he was the official adult with the pass. And then, we'd go out of the security gate and Ruth would be waiting. Would Andrew be there too?

I played with my earring and bit back my smile.

The stewardess called the first boarding group, and I hugged Mom and Dad.

"Be safe, Sades," Dad said.

"And call us the minute you meet up with Rick," Mom said.

"Okay. I love you guys."

They both hugged me again, and then Dad checked me in with the stewardess in charge. She helped me to my seat, and hefted my baggage into the overhead bin.

I took out my sketchbook and pencils, which I'd kept in my smaller bag, and drew the view outside my window of the baggage trucks and various runways. Nothing else around me caught my interest, and I kept thinking of Charlotte's hair flying every which way around her face as she was in the middle of landing on the Chinese jump rope. Even though she had so much to be afraid of, in that moment, light seemed to stream out of each strand of her hair and the tips of her fingers. She'd been filled with joy. I drew quickly, but my pencils could only create the shape and expression. Maybe when I was in Owl Creek, I'd ask Vivian to use her paints to put the picture into color, the way it should be.

After the airline attendants did their safety talk, we rolled to the runway, and the engines fired up. I folded my arms tight and tried not to look nervous. These first few minutes of a flight and the landing always made my heart leap around like a fish desperate to get back into water. As long as I didn't think too hard about how much a plane must weigh, and the fact that it was only held up by momentum and air pressure, I could usually calm myself down. But Dad had always been there before to give my shoulder a reassuring squeeze, too. This time, if I looked too pale, one of the attendants would think I wasn't brave enough to fly on my own, and I really, really didn't want them to think that. I was fine, really.

Please, don't let the plane fall from the sky.

I closed my eyes and breathed. I'd been asking God for a lot of things lately. Was that selfish of me? To think about God whenever I felt overwhelmed or at the end of my options? In many of his youth group talks, Doug had said God never gives you more than you can handle. Maybe that, more than the Karl ambush last night, was why I'd suddenly found myself here, on a plane, on my way to Owl Creek. I needed to talk, and sort out my questions. I needed to talk to Ruth and Vivian and Frankie. I needed to figure out how to stop messing everything up.

Would my life always be falling apart? Last year, in Owl Creek, the mess had been different. My problems had mostly been inside me. But now, it seemed like all the problems were outside me, and even more out of my control. What was I supposed to do about Pippa, Karl, Cici, the girls? No matter what I did, I couldn't really change the way things seemed to be playing out.

The popping in my ears stopped, and outside my window, a thick blanket of clouds stretched to the horizon. My heartbeat slowed, and I turned to a new page in my sketchbook, not sure what to draw next. Charlotte's sleepy voice came back to me. She had asked me to tell her a story about feeling God come close. Thinking about it now, I hadn't felt that closeness, practically at all, since I'd left Owl Creek. Was I doing something wrong? Had something changed?

I started sketching, trying to relax into the feeling of stroke and line, letting my hand and my heart think for me, giving my mind a rest. I'd been thinking so hard lately, and it hadn't seemed to get me anywhere.

A small island appeared in the center of my page, surrounded by water. One palm tree, heavy with coconuts, gave shade to a girl sitting at its base. Me. The island's shore was littered with glass bottles, each with paper inside, as though every message-in-a-bottle that had been thrown out to sea had ended up here, on this island.

I turned the page and drew three boxes in a vertical line, wanting to show a sequence of action, like I'd been doing with my doors. In the first, the girl chose a bottle. Next, she read the paper. Here, I paused. What would be on the paper? People sent wishes out to sea and sometimes questions, or even notes to people they loved but couldn't speak to directly. The way you could pray, and sometimes you felt God come near, and other times you felt like you were throwing a bottle out to sea, and who knew whether God would hear you, or you'd hear him.

If I was honest with myself, I didn't really believe that. I knew God heard my prayers. How could I doubt that, after all I'd learned and been through this year? Still, I felt like I was missing a connection, too. I didn't want to throw my prayers out to sea like messages in a bottle. There had to be a better way.

I drew the third picture, a close up of the note, clutched in the girl's hands. *Are you out there?*

As I shaded the hands, my pencil slowed and then stopped, a realization slipping into my hand, up my arm, wrapping around my heart and then finally coming clear in my mind. The girl is on the island, not God. The bottles aren't messages from the girl to God; they are messages from God to the girl. And she's out there, alone, with no better way of communicating than gathering messages from bottles. I stared at the seat back, trying to understand.

Don't think. Draw.

Yes, my mind had totally failed me so far.

The stewardess asked me a question, but it took me a second to make sense of her words, as I returned to myself, here in the airplane, traveling alone, on my way to Owl Creek.

"Um, yeah. Thanks. Coke, please."

I put my sketchbook in the seat back pocket, and she handed me a glass of ice, a napkin, and a can of Coke. "Peanuts, cookies, or pretzels?"

"Cookies."

I hardly tasted the cookies, because I was so focused on figuring out the story. If the girl was alone on the island, how had she gotten there? And how would she get home? And would she find a better way to talk to God than through messages in bottles?

When I finished my Coke and my cookies, my brain felt dizzy, like I'd spun and spun on the same questions for too long. Maybe I'd take a nap and finish the story later, when I'd had more time. Not to think, but maybe to listen? I put my tray table up, leaned my seat back and slipped instantly to sleep.

"Ladies and gentlemen ..." A voice over the intercom woke me up.

I sat up and stretched my neck.

"...We are making our final descent. Please put your tray tables up and your seats in the upright position."

Ruth's dad would be waiting at the gate, and Ruth would be just outside security. And maybe other people would come too. I sat up straight and felt my hair. Probably I was a mess after having slept so long, but I couldn't redo my hair without wetting it down. When we got on the ground, I could dig out my lip-gloss and mints, so at least I wouldn't have bad breath.

Outside the window, the runway neared, and I grabbed the arms of my chair, holding tight. We only bounced once, and the plane slowed without much trouble. I had to wait until everyone else was out before the stewardess could come help me with my bag, but that gave me a minute to take care of the breath situation. Rick waited at the desk, grinning, and gave me one of his signature bear hugs.

"Sadie, I'm so glad you're here!"

I hugged him back. "Is Ruth here?"

He reached for the handle of my bag. "Yep. There's a surprise waiting for you outside security."

I tried not to hope too much that the surprise would include Andrew. After I called my parents to let them know I was safe, Rick waited for me outside the restroom while I did battle with my hair. With wet, but more orderly braids, I followed Rick through the long airport halls toward the exit.

Chapter 19

Homecoming

"**S**urprise!"

Everyone had come—Vivian, Frankie, Ruth, her brother and sister, Ruth's mom, Andrew, Helen, even Penny. They'd worn clown wigs for the occasion and held up colorful signs reading "Welcome home, Sadie!" Penny hadn't needed to wear a clown wig—her hair was dyed a spectacular shade of lime green.

Home. This did feel like coming home, in lots of ways. They swept me into hug after hug, and finally, after feeling like I'd been passed around a whole dance floor of people, I found myself hugging Andrew.

He whispered in my ear, "Missed you, Sades."

I stepped back and smiled at him, realizing he'd grown about an inch since I'd last seen him. Now I had to look up to see his eyes.

They'd come in three cars, and we decided we'd all go out to eat, even though it was already eight o'clock in Michigan. I still needed to eat, and Penny said she wouldn't mind some chocolate cake for dessert.

Dinner was a whirlwind of everyone talking over everyone else, and so much laughter my stomach ached. After everything that had been happening, I felt like I'd suddenly left a very dark room and walked into the sunshine. As the adults paid the bill, I realized I was also bone-deep exhausted.

Andrew laced his fingers through mine and squeezed my hand on the way out to the car. "Call me tomorrow. I want to take you to see July and her cubs."

"No, we have an art lesson tomorrow," Frankie said, wrapping her arm around my waist.

Ruth made a face. "You guys, she's staying with me. I have first dibs."

"Give her room to breathe," Rick said. "There's plenty of time for everyone to see Sadie."

Yes. I'd come with a one-way ticket, and no one knew how long I'd stay. Even with all the happiness, that felt strange. My family in California, me here, for who knew how long.

I promised I'd call everyone and make plans, and then joined Ruth in the back seat of their SUV. Hannah and Mark fell asleep almost as soon as they were buckled in, and I felt myself nodding off too.

When the engine stopped, I woke up and we all trundled off to bed. Since Ruth's family had an official guest bedroom, I had my own room. Tonight, since I wasn't sure I could put two more words together even to say goodnight, my own room was perfect. The minute I slipped under the covers and my head hit the pillow, I was asleep.

"Sadie, Sadie, Sadie!"

I woke up to what felt like an earthquake, but what was actually Hannah and Mark jumping on my bed.

"Dad made waffles!" Hannah shouted.

"Mark and Hannah," Ruth's voice was stern from the doorway. "What did I say about waking Sadie up?"

"But it's time for breakfast," Hannah said, pouting, as she climbed down off the bed.

"And that's a reason to pounce on her in her sleep?"

"Sorry, Sadie," Mark said, looking shamefaced, but only a little.

When I sat up, Mark gave me a wide-eyed look. "Whoa!"

I reached up for my hair. Yep, wild. It always was when I woke up.

Making crazy eyes at Mark, I said, "Better watch out! I'm a monster in the morning."

He shrieked and raced Hannah out of the room.

"I'm supposed to babysit the monsters this morning," Ruth said. "And I guess Frankie and Vivian are going to be having an art lesson. You want to go over there and avoid the mad crazy kids, and then we can go to Black Bear Java for ice cream later, when Mom finishes her volunteer fair at the church?"

"Sounds perfect." I didn't feel up to making decisions or plans of my own yet.

Ruth came to sit with me on the bed. "Are you okay?"

From her expression, I knew she really wanted to know.

"There's a lot going on back home, with Pips, and the girls, and of course with Dad's case. I know I can't avoid it all forever, but when they offered to send me here, I didn't complain. I wanted to see all of you, and I needed a break, too."

"Were you scared? Of the guy following you?"

"Yeah," I admitted. "I wanted to stand up to him, to tell him he was wrong, because Charlotte really needs that test, and Karl's only getting in the way of Tyler finishing it. But when I saw him, I was too afraid to say anything at all."

"It's not your job to stand up to a crazy guy," Ruth said.

"I know, you're right. I just wish there was something I could do to help Charlotte."

After breakfast, Ruth's mom drove me over to Vivian's trailer. Construction was in full steam on her house, and they'd already finished the wooden frame. Workers swarmed the lot, nailing, cutting, shouting to one another, and using power tools. The trailer was parked in the trees near the back of the lot. We picked our way over, and knocked on the door.

"She's here!" Frankie shouted when she threw open the door.

"I'll pick you up at two," Annabelle told me.

Frankie laid out the pages across the table. She'd mostly

166

worked in collage, where Vivian had drawn in pastel, colored pencil, and charcoal, and I'd mostly painted. We had about thirty pages in all.

"The sketchbook has eighty pages," Frankie said. "7 have to get moving."

"I like how we've used so many different mediums," Vivian said. "But I think we need to find some other visual ideas. We have a lot of literal doors."

"If we could use words, or write a story, it might be easier," I said.

"There's no reason we can't use words in an image," Vivian said. "But we might be still thinking too literally."

"Your puddle isn't literal," Frankie said.

"Right," Vivian said. "So, here's the challenge. I want you to head outside and find something that is definitely not a door, but that you can imagine being a door. And then we'll all come back in and create a new piece of art."

Frankie and I were halfway out when Vivian called, "And don't forget to take a cookie with you."

I laughed and took a still warm chocolate chip cookie from the tray. Frankie did too, and followed me out into the warm summer afternoon. Tall grass tickled my bare legs as I walked away from the workers, out toward the trees.

I had just finished my last bite of cookie, halfway across the field when Frankie said, "Watch out for ticks."

Frankie was wearing full-length jeans, much more appropriate than my cut-off shorts.

"Yeah, I was just thinking that," I said.

I'd only been in California for a few weeks, and I'd already forgotten some very important Michigan basics. No matter where you went, if there was the possibility you might go outside, you ought to cover your skin.

Now that I was thinking about ticks, my skin crawled and itched, as though they were swarming me. I shuddered and ran the rest of the way to the forest, where the grass thinned out. I planted myself in the middle of the path and started inspecting for black creepy crawlies.

Frankie caught up to me, laughing. "Do you have an infestation?"

"Very funny." I brushed off my legs, pretty sure I was tick-free. "You don't see any, do you?"

Frankie circled me, and then stopped, looking close at the back of my knee. "Wait."

"Wait, what?" My heart raced, and I could hear the blood pounding in my ears. You'd think such a small bug couldn't cause panic like this. "Tell me, Frankie!"

"Sheesh," Frankie said, elbowing me. "I'm just teasing."

I rolled my eyes at her and started down the path. Anything could be a door, but I didn't just want to find some random leaf and call it a door. I wanted to actually see a door in whatever object I picked, maybe have an idea of what might be on the other side. Frankie didn't seem to be having any luck either.

"Have you heard from your mom?" I asked her.

Instead of answering, she sat on a stump and picked at the peeling bark.

"Frankie? Is everything okay?"

Finally, she looked up at me. "They're getting a divorce."

I hadn't realized her parents weren't divorced already. They'd been living apart for a long time, and Frankie's mom had a long-term boyfriend.

"Chase and mom want to get married, so she finally needs to make their separation official."

I found a stump of my own to sit on, and waited for her to say more. I couldn't read her emotions on her face. Mostly, she just looked blank.

"Nothing is changing, really," Frankie said. "But as part of the divorce, they have to decide what to do with me."

"What to do with you?" As though she was an old couch that no one wanted anymore.

"They want me to decide. Now that I've been in New York, and here with Dad." She looked up at me with watery eyes.

"Do you have to decide on one or the other? Couldn't you spend some time with each?"

"Maybe? I don't know. I'm confused. Before I went to New York, I wouldn't have even had to think about the question. I wanted to live with Dad, period. But, even though Mom insists on calling me Francesca, and even though she's a little . . . " Frankie looked up at me and memories from my trip to New York with her flashed between us. She choked back a laugh. " . . . Okay, *very* ridiculous sometimes, she kind of grew on me. And Dad plans to move to Canada permanently, so going with him means moving again. You know how fun that is."

Silence settled between us. Probably I should say something, give some wise advice. But as I searched for something, anything, to say, I came up blank.

"It's okay, Sadie," Frankie said, breaking the silence. "I don't expect you to tell me what to do."

When I looked up at her, I saw a familiar expression, one I'd felt on my own face a lot recently, but that I hadn't really thought about. Guilt. But neither she nor I had anything to feel guilty about, right? Unless . . .

"Are you sure you don't know what you want?" I asked slowly, realizing that I was asking the question of myself just as much as I was asking it of Frankie. "Or are you worried about hurting someone's feelings?"

Frankie pried the chunk of bark that she'd been working on off of the stump all together and tossed it into the trees. Then, she locked eyes with me.

"Terrified," she said.

Only one word, but it nearly stopped my heart. And I knew, as though someone had finally hit me over the head, that I was terrified too. Not of Karl or being caught for bullying or cheating, but because I did know what I wanted. I did know how I felt, and no amount of insisting that I didn't know what to do could change that fact. Just the thought of speaking up made my heart drum in my chest.

"Do you want to talk about it?" Frankie asked.

I shook my head no. "Mine's nothing like yours. I . . . We'll talk about it sometime."

"Okay." She brushed bark off her jeans and then gestured grandly. "Then, shall we look for doors?"

I grinned at her imitation of her mom and then caught her arm and pulled her into a hug. "Thank you, Frankie."

She squeezed back. "You too, Sades."

Chapter 20

Listening

We searched for a while, but probably because we were each caught up in our own thoughts, we didn't find anything.

Frankie stopped and nudged me. "You're not looking."

"Neither are you."

"Okay." She scanned the forest and pointed at a deep, dark knot in a tree. "What about that?"

Promising. I went closer to take a look, and I liked it, but it still didn't feel quite right. I turned back to tell Frankie so, but she'd moved on, crouching over something on the path.

I hurried over. "What did you find?"

An old baseball card lay on the ground, its edges curled and dirty.

"I'm trying to imagine whether this would be the kind of door that would turn on its hinges, or if it would be the kind of door that you'd jump into feet first, like the chalk pictures in Mary Poppins."

"What's on the other side?" I asked.

"Dirt," Frankie said.

I raised an eyebrow at her.

"Okay. I guess an old-time baseball stadium. Maybe it's a time travel card that takes you back to the minute when this player was making the play they've drawn on this card."

"I like it." Now I really had to come up with something cool.

"I'm going back in to draw," Frankie said. "See you in a minute."

I wandered further down the path, remembering how I'd found an old pocket watch out here in this forest. It had belonged to Vivian's husband a long time ago. Probably the baseball card had belonged to Vivian's son, Peter. There had to be something else out here, something interesting. As I looked, my mind wandered back to thoughts of the girls, and Karl. The thing was, right now, as long as I was in Owl Creek, I couldn't do anything. It didn't make sense to play scenes over and over in my head, what it would be like to face the girls, the expressions on their faces. Or to tell Pips how I really felt. And I may not even have the chance to speak up again to Karl.

I am with you. You are never alone.

The words, sudden and sweet, slowed my heartbeat. Too often, I forgot. I started to think I had to figure everything out, or drum up the courage inside myself to handle my problems all on my own. I forgot to ask for help.

What if I don't know what to say? I asked.

When it's time, the right words will come.

I didn't so much hear the words as feel them, vibrating through me, rich and soothing and warm. With the words came the realization that I should come back to now, this moment in the forest, to my small task of finding a door.

Be present. You never know what this exact moment will bring.

I was nearing the bridge that spanned the creek. Out of habit, I found a stick to toss into the water. Andrew and I loved to play this game — Sink the Boat. The idea was that you threw the stick into the water, and then tried to hit it with a rock enough times to sink the boat before it floated downstream and out of reach.

I sat on the bridge, and tossed the stick out through the railing, watching the stick dance and spin in the current. When the stick passed between two rocks, a tiny waterfall sucked the stick down out of sight. I leaned my forehead against the post in front of me, thinking, trying to listen. I had no idea why God would care about me drawing door-ways, but maybe even tiny things were important to God. Maybe there was something I was meant to see.

Suddenly, I sat up and jumped to my feet. I found another stick, aimed carefully, and watched this time as the current took it, swallowing the stick whole in the same place where the other stick had gone down.

If you were a teeny-tiny creature, and that stick was your boat, then under the waterfall, you'd have some kind of watery adventure, right? Not drowning. But what if underneath there were caverns that you could sail through, and on the banks there were treasures to find? It would be like finding out the world as you knew it, the stream, suddenly had another level, more depth and adventure and challenge than you ever realized. And you might even realize, like what always happened in my favorite books that you, yourself, had an important mission, something that only you could do.

"Something that only I can do," I whispered.

I was tempted to think about this question, study all the angles, force an answer to come clear. What could I do that no one else could? But I reminded myself to stay in the moment, to do what I needed to do right now. Draw. I closed my eyes and pictured the images. They'd be a sequence of three, like Vivian's puddle drawing. Or maybe I'd even draw more frames, maybe a whole page full, to show the creature on the boat, the boat going under, and then the adventure beyond. I took off running for Vivian's trailer.

When I burst inside, I had to stop and double over to catch my breath.

"You okay, Sadie?" Vivian asked.

"Come see, Sadie!" Frankie motioned me over to the table, where she'd already penciled in the collage of the card and the baseball stadium beneath. "I think I'm going to try to do the entire image with baseball magazines and baseball cards."

"She already called her dad to come pick her up so she can go buy supplies," Vivian said.

"I can't wait to see how it will come out. Is that okay with you, though, Sadie?"

"Yes, of course!" I knew how it felt to be on a roll and want to just keep going.

I sat in the chair next to Frankie and started sketching out my idea. Eventually, I'd probably do it in paint, because water was difficult for me to draw, but in paint the texture and smoothness and motion of the stream would come clear.

I'd finished an outline of three frames by the time Frankie's dad honked outside.

"See you soon, Sadie?" Frankie asked.

"I think Ruth and I are going to youth group on Thursday," I said. "Are you coming?"

"Actually, they're having a progressive dinner scavenger hunt thing tomorrow night," Frankie said. "Even I was invited."

I laughed. "Even you?"

Frankie swatted at me and then closed her sketchbook. "Well, I'm not exactly an official member of the group."

"You mean you don't have the secret card?" I teased. "Okay, then, I'll see you tomorrow at the progressive dinner scavenger hunt thing, whatever that means."

Frankie grinned. "Try to convince Viv to come, too."

She waved and hurried out the door. Vivian poured herself another cup of tea, refilled the cookie plate from the batch she'd just taken out of the oven, and brought it over to the table. She watched me draw the fourth frame, and then as I started drawing the next box, she pointed to my second frame.

"I like that you zoomed in here, really close, to show her slipping into the water. You feel like you're being swallowed into the picture, the same way the water is swallowing her. Have you been playing with drawing in sequences like this recently?"

"Your drawing of the puddle started me thinking about it, and then the kids at camp have been drawing picture books, and I've been talking to them about drawings that go in order, and telling stories."

I flipped back a page to show her my drawings of the island, pointing out my picture with the close up on the note. "Sometimes it makes sense to zoom in, right?"

"Right." Vivian nodded, studying my images. "So what are you drawing here?"

"I'm not sure," I admitted. "On the plane, I got the idea of writing and drawing a picture book of my own. I know that this character is stuck on the island, and that she's found all these messages in bottles, but I don't know how to help her off the island."

"What does this mean, 'Are you out there?'"

I felt my cheeks reddening, and I wanted to just toss out an *I don't know,* but then I felt a tiny inner nudge.

Now. Try it now.

I didn't have to ask what this meant. I did know, and speaking up to Vivian shouldn't be difficult. Still, my mouth felt cotton-dry as I tried to form the words.

"I thought the girl was tossing out messages in the bottle to God, to try to be heard. But when I realized what was on the note, I ..." I had to pause, gather my courage. "... Saw that God was sending the messages in the only way he could. She'd traveled or lost her way or whatever, all the way out to that small island, with no other way to communicate. And yet he didn't give up. He kept sending messages, even if he had to toss them out to the sea in bottles."

Vivian studied my face. "And you think that's you? Stuck on an island with no good way to communicate?"

"I don't know. Maybe?" The words slipped out before I could stop myself. But this time, I knew I wasn't hiding behind them. I really didn't know, and I needed to admit that to someone.

"If you could say anything at all, what would you say?" Vivian asked.

I turned back to the drawing of the creature on the stick-boat, the watery world she was entering, her head held high. "When I was out at the creek, I thought of this story, about a creature who slips beneath the creek's surface and finds there's something more going on, all underneath her ordinary world. And she is given a quest, something important to do, so she knows she matters, she's unique."

Even though I hadn't connected my answer to her question, Vivian just waited, sipped her tea, and gave me space to think out loud.

"Everything is a mess, and none of it makes sense. I don't know how to fix any of the problems, and I feel like even if

I did speak up, or do something, it wouldn't matter. I don't know how to make a difference. I feel so ... small." As the word came out, I finally understood, felt the truth drop deep down inside me, painful, heavy, but solid too. "I want to do something, but I don't know what I'm supposed to do."

Tears spilled down my cheeks, and Vivian hurried to find some tissues. She handed me the box. I tried to control them, but the tears kept coming.

"Lots of times I don't know what to do either," Vivian said. "I feel like I should do something big, flashy, significant, something that will fix everything once and for all. But the truth is, we usually help in tiny little steps. Like your drawings. You are finding answers one at a time, like tiny pearls, that you will eventually string together."

"But what if it's too late?" I choked back a sob. "What if Cici dies and Charlotte gets sick too and—"

"The trouble with tiny steps is that you can't see the whole picture until later, after the fact. And you can't take tiny steps if you focus on the big problems. They freeze us in our tracks."

I smiled a watery smile. "So I need to think small?"

Vivian took my hand. "Think now. Keep listening. I can see that God is speaking to you through your drawings, and he's moving you toward something. If you really want to know what to do, consider starting there. Start with what you've been given so far."

Even though this wasn't the fix-everything kind of answer I wanted, Vivian's words were like gentle hands on my shoulders, turning me toward a path that might actually make things better. My breathing calmed, and I dried my cheeks with a tissue.

"Okay. I can do that," I said.

Vivian broke into a wide smile. "I have no doubt. Now, you know what the right thing to do this second is?"

"What?"

She nudged the cookie plate toward me. "Eat cookies."

I laughed and grabbed a cookie, which was still warm.

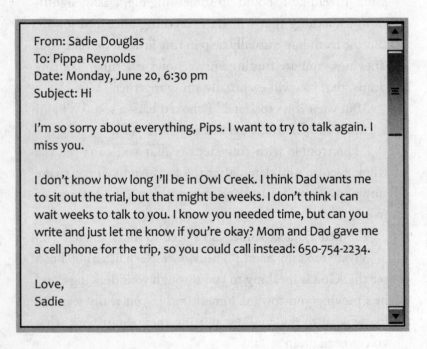

From: Sadie Douglas
To: Pippa Reynolds
Date: Monday, June 20, 6:30 pm
Subject: Hi

I'm so sorry about everything, Pips. I want to try to talk again. I miss you.

I don't know how long I'll be in Owl Creek. I think Dad wants me to sit out the trial, but that might be weeks. I don't think I can wait weeks to talk to you. I know you needed time, but can you write and just let me know if you're okay? Mom and Dad gave me a cell phone for the trip, so you could call instead: 650-754-2234.

Love,
Sadie

Spirit Bear

Andrew pushed a branch aside so I could pass under. Even though the day was hot, in the shade, the forest was still cool from last night's dew. Birds called here and there, but otherwise, the forest was silent. We tried to keep our footsteps light so we wouldn't frighten the bears.

"We've seen July with her cubs in this part of the forest," Andrew whispered. "She doesn't mind my mom or I, as long as we keep a reasonable distance."

Had anyone told me a year ago I'd be out creeping through the forest looking for bears, I'd never have believed them. But I'd learned that black bears were really gentle creatures at heart, beautiful, wild, to be respected and given their distance, certainly, but amazing, too.

I'd settle for seeing any bear, but I was hoping to see the spirit bear, who was still only a cub. I'd been the first to spot her, astonishing Helen with the news. The all-white bears, called spirit bears, were one-in-a-million cubs born to black bears. Also, they were hardly ever seen outside of Canada, so to see a spirit bear here, in Michigan, was a doubly big deal.

But it hadn't been the unusualness that had frozen me in my steps the day I saw the white bear cub. It had been the quiet. The way time slowed down as she looked me straight in the eyes, like the long breathless moments while you watch an eclipse. Just like today, I'd been far from calm then. And I wanted that feeling again, the cotton-soft peace that slips deep down inside after you've seen something astonishing. I couldn't stand to keep feeling the way I did now, brambly, like my insides were filled with the thorny vines that we battled to get deeper into the forest.

As we stepped into a clearing where the trees thinned out, and sun pooled in patches across a grassy area, Andrew held out an arm. "This is the place."

We picked our way over to a fallen log and sat down.

"They like to eat those wild blackberries over there," Andrew said. "And the cubs romp around and play chase between the trees. Probably they're watching us from somewhere nearby, deciding if it's safe to come out."

"Will they come out with me here?"

"Hard to say. I never know what they'll do," Andrew said.

We sat for a few moments in silence, watching the edges of the clearing for any sign of movement. I heard a scrabbling sound, which might be bear claws clambering down a tree trunk. I tilted my head toward the sound and raised an eyebrow at Andrew. He nodded and put his finger to his lips.

A few seconds later, two cubs bounded into the clearing. The first, the black bear, tumbled into a somersault in a patch of ivy, and then started wiggling around on his back, the way Higgins sometimes did when he had an itch. The other, the spirit bear, had been chasing him, and couldn't stop fast enough. She tumbled over him and they rolled over and over, batting at one another with their paws. July stepped watchfully into the clearing and looked our way.

"Hey bear," Andrew said, in the singsong way his mom did when she was approaching a bear in the forest. "Hey July."

She watched us for a moment, and then circled the perimeter of the clearing, her eyes mostly fixed on her cubs.

"Do the cubs have names yet?" I whispered.

"We've been calling them Salt and Pepper."

"Really? A spirit bear? Salt? Doesn't seem quite right."

"She doesn't look too serious right now, though, does she?" Andrew asked.

Salt and Pepper were now playing some kind of tag-game, but it was unclear who "it" was. One minute, Salt was chasing and the next, Pepper was on her tail. Whatever the rules were, they were clearly having fun.

I felt Andrew watching me, and realized I'd been spinning my star earring round and round.

"You still have them," he said, as I turned to him.

I raised an eyebrow, teasing to try to lighten the mood. "What, did you think I'd throw them away?"

He laced his fingers through mine. "Sadie, I know trying to ... I don't know. Be something particular ..."

I couldn't help smiling. He sounded so much like me, circling the far edges of what he wanted to say, not able to just spit it out.

Somehow, finding words to help him was easier than trying to say them for myself. "You mean boyfriend and girlfriend?"

"Um, yeah." He cleared his throat. "Well, I know that's hard, since we're so far away from one another. And next year, when I'm in Minnesota ..."

"Pretty unlikely my dad will ship me off to Minnesota, right?"

"Yeah."

We sat, looking at our hands, his tan fingers dark against my pale skin.

"The thing is," Andrew finally went on, "when you send me an email, or, well, you've never called me or anything, but if you did, when I hear from you, or see you, I just feel ..."

I pulled together all of my courage and looked him straight in the eye and he looked back, neither of us looking away.

"It's like when you're balancing on a log, walking across a creek," I said. "And you're fine, you're not going to fall. But if someone comes along and takes your hand, you feel more ..."

"Steady." He finished for me. "Like even though lots of things might be wrong, overall, you're okay."

I could feel my heartbeat everywhere, in my fingers laced through his, in my shoulders, my arms, my legs, even in my toes.

He held my hand up to his lips and brushed a kiss across my fingertips. Then, he gave me that crooked smile I loved so much.

"Just promise me you'll keep emailing. And I'll email too. Or call. And maybe someday ..."

His voice trailed off and someday hung in the air between us, hopeful, sending a shiver through me.

"Are you cold?" he asked, wrapping his arm around me.

"No," I whispered, snuggling in close.

We sat there like that for a long time, watching the bear cubs tumble and play. Eventually, we'd have to get up and go to the progressive dinner, but right then, I let time stop.

Chapter 22

The Call

"Gather round, everyone!" Penny stood on top of the picnic table outside the Tree House, and motioned us all to circle up.

Everyone had shown up: Frankie, Ruth, the twins, her parents, Vivian, Andrew, Helen, the entire youth group, and even some other people from town. Since Doug was gone for the summer, Penny had taken over, and she had been running wild events every week, according to Ruth. This week was a competition, and the prize was a year's worth of free ice cream at Black Bear Java for the winning team. How Penny had weaseled the Black Bear Java owners into giving this prize was beyond me. Still, Penny seemed to have a special way with people. Maybe her glow-in-the-dark hair mesmerized them.

"So here's the scoop," Penny said. "You'll work in teams

of four. Each team will be given the first clue at the same time. Work out the clue, and then head out to where you think the first course is waiting. Once you arrive, you'll be given the second clue to work out while you wait for the other teams to arrive. We'll all eat, and then you'll be allowed to take off for the next clue in the order you arrived. We'll stagger your departures by three minutes, so the first team will have a three-minute head start on their way to the second clue. You'll earn points for your order of arrival at each of the six courses. Whichever team ends up with the most points is the winner."

"Can we start on the ice cream today?" Ted asked.

Ruth elbowed me and I choked back a laugh.

Penny laughed, too. "If you're still hungry after six courses, Ted, and if your team wins, then yes, you can start on the ice cream today."

"Break into teams of four, then," Penny said, "And I'll bring around envelopes."

I had wanted to be on a team with Andrew, Ruth, Frankie and Vivian, but since we could only have four on the team, Vivian went with Helen and a couple other adults.

Ruth's family made a team together, and her dad shouted over at her, "Better watch out, Ruth! We'll all be eating ice cream and you'll just have to watch."

"Ha ha!" she shouted back.

Penny passed out the envelopes, and once we all had them, we opened on the count of three.

Here music played beneath the trees

Now hear only the wind's melodies

"That's it?" Frankie asked.

Ruth silently read the clue again and then looked up at us. "Any ideas?"

In May, Vivian had showed me a piano tucked away in a remote part of the forest, but that was all the way out by Hiawatha. They hadn't expected teams to drive, had they?

"The abandoned piano?" I shrugged. "The one in the trees?"

"But that's all the way in Hiawatha!" Andrew said.

"Shhhh!" Frankie and Ruth both warned.

Ruth motioned us all closer, and whispered, "I don't think Penny would make us drive, since she allowed some teams to not have an adult. But what about the musical? There were all those scenes scattered through the forest."

"But there were six different places," I said. "If we start out for one, everyone will get the idea, and who knows if we'll get to the right one first?"

Ruth looked around at the other teams. "They're all just as stumped as we are. And probably that's what they meant to have happen for this first clue, since we'll all take off at the same time."

"Does the wind mean anything?" Frankie asked. "I know I wasn't here for the musical, but since the clue is so short, maybe one of the scenes had something to do with wind? Or one of the places is windier than the others?"

Andrew locked eyes with me, and we both knew. One of his lines at the end of the show had been about how the girl's song joined the music of the wind through the trees. He'd hated the line because he couldn't remember the exact wording, and we'd had to work and work on it to get it just right.

"You know, don't you?" Frankie asked.

We both nodded.

"Let's make a run for it, then," Ruth said. "Don't say anything out loud because someone might hear you. Just run and we'll follow."

"Are you sure we shouldn't meander? Like we're not sure?" Frankie asked.

We all glanced around at the other groups. Lots of them looked like they were coming to a decision, ready to move.

"Nope, this time we'd better run," Andrew said. "Ready, set ... go!"

We sprinted across the field toward the area of forest where we'd played the last scene. I could hear people shouting and a few others starting to run, too, but we had a head start. Halfway to the trees, my lungs felt like they would explode, but I forced myself to keep up with Andrew. Finally, when I felt like I would trip over my feet and fall on my face, or die from lack of oxygen, we burst into the trees and doubled over, gasping for breath. Seconds later, Helen, Vivian, and their group joined us, with Ted's group right behind.

Penny had set up tall round tables where we could stand and eat, with bright colored tablecloths and flowerpots with Gerber daisies for centerpieces. She handed out envelopes in the order we arrived and we huddled up again to study our clue.

Boxes, tape, bows and ribbons
Here great gifts were shown and given

We all knew immediately. The caretaker's cabin, where we'd given Christmas to the Thompson family. As we studied the faces of the other teams, we saw they knew too. Hopefully some of Penny's clues were a little harder, or we'd be neck in neck the whole way.

Every team had arrived at the first course area within minutes, and Penny climbed onto a large stump. "The first course, an appetizer, is Ants on a Log!"

"I'm not eating ants!" Ted shouted, but Penny jumped down to uncover trays of celery sticks, filled with peanut butter, and dotted with raisins. Three waitresses, dressed in overalls and plaid shirts, with their hair in pigtails or braids, wearing straw hats, came out of the trees, and started passing through the group with trays, handing out napkins and celery sticks.

When we'd all had our fill, Penny gave us the go ahead. "All right, Frankie's team, you're first. Go!"

We took off running, this time at a slower pace because we knew we'd arrive at the cabin before anyone else with a three-minute head start.

Picnic blankets had been laid out in the cabin's front yard. We sat down and Andrew picked up the envelope that had already been placed on the blanket ahead of time. Just then, my phone rang. I jumped, not used to the sound.

"You have a phone?" Ruth asked. "I didn't know that!"

"Only for emergencies."

Which meant this was an emergency. I stood up and walked a few feet away to answer.

"Hello?"

Pippa's voice crackled over the line. My first thought was that I must not have a good connection. My second thought was ... What? Pippa's calling me? I hadn't expected her to actually call. I'd thought she'd email first. Maybe she was so upset she couldn't write me. I braced myself for the worst.

"Sadie, are you there?" she asked again.

"Hi, Pips," I said.

"Sadie, you have to come home."

"I have to what?"

"Charlotte asked for you all day at camp. Cici is a lot worse, Sades. I think she's dying. Charlotte needs you."

I stopped breathing.

In the background, I could hear Alexis' voice. "Pippa, what are you doing? Are you on the phone?"

"I have to go, Sadie. I wasn't supposed to call you. Just ... just figure out a way to come home. Okay? Please?"

The line went dead. She must have hung up just as her mom came into the room.

I stood there for a minute, looking at the cabin, trying to absorb the news, trying to start breathing again. Cici might be dying? Charlotte needed me. And even though so much was wrong between us, Pippa had called. I scanned my friends' worried faces. Andrew. Frankie. Ruth. I'd just gotten here. Now, I was supposed to turn around and go home? The thought made me feel sick. I could still feel the soft brush of Andrew's lips against my fingertips. How could I leave, knowing this might be the last time I'd see him? I'd see Ruth again at the end of the summer, but depending on where Frankie went, I might never see her either.

I walked slowly back to join the group on the blanket as Helen's team charged up, pouncing on a blanket and ripping open the clue.

"Everything okay, Sadie?" Andrew asked.

"It's ..." Once again, I was crying, and I couldn't stop the tears. I swiped at them angrily. "No."

Immediately, Ruth and Frankie were at my sides, each with a hand on my shoulder.

I shook my head, trying to find words, any words. "Cici is dying."

Even though they didn't know who Cici was, their faces fell, all three of them. I felt them squeeze in tighter, Andrew gripping my hand, the girls holding my shoulders.

"What can we do to help?" Ruth asked. "Who called?"

"Pippa."

"I'll find tissues." Ruth ran for the cabin.

Helen and Vivian came over.

"Sadie, what is it?" Vivian asked.

"I need to call my parents."

When Ruth came back with tissues, I sopped up my tears and blew my nose. Then, I convinced them to let me go back into the forest on my own. I needed space to talk to my parents.

I dialed our house and waited. Dad picked up.

"Hello?" he said, his voice laced with tension.

"Dad."

He must have heard in the way I said his name that I knew, because he didn't say anything right away. When he finally spoke, he said, "Oh, Sadie."

"Dad, Charlotte is asking for me. I have to come home."

"How do you—"

"Pips told me. I know she wasn't supposed to, but Dad, if Charlotte needs me, I should come."

"Sadie, we just sent you to Owl Creek. You can't keep flying back and forth across the country."

"I know. I know if I come home I have to stay. But I have to come, Dad. Please."

"I don't want you here during the trial, Sadie. It's too much pressure. You just ..."

"I just need to come home, Dad. For Charlotte."

"For Charlotte," Dad repeated. "What are you going to do, Sades? You can't ..."

"I know I can't fix anything, Dad, and I don't know what I'll do, but I have to be there for her. Please."

A long silence followed, and I could almost hear Dad weighing the options. Of course, he'd rather I stayed in Owl Creek where I was safe, where I didn't have to face Karl, or Cici's death for that matter. I knew he wanted to protect me from all of it.

"Dad," I spoke into the silence. "You know how sometimes there's something you just have to do?"

Dad blew out a sigh. "Yes."

"This is like that, Dad. I need to come home."

After another long pause, Dad sighed again. "All right, Sades. Pack your bags. I'll call Ruth's dad and make the arrangements."

The impossible had happened. Dad had agreed to let me come home. But as I walked back to tell Andrew and Ruth and Frankie, my body was still heavy with dread. Leaving Owl Creek now would be at least ten times as hard as it had been the first time. I stopped just before I stepped back out of the trees, gathering myself.

You are not alone.

Yes. After everything, I'd almost forgotten that I didn't have to do this, any of it, on my own. And that made all the difference.

I closed my eyes and whispered, *Please help me.*

Chapter 23

Trust Me

I stuffed my last shirt into the suitcase, zipped it up, and sat down on the guest room bed next to Ruth. "I'm sorry we lost the competition."

"Like anyone's worried about that," Ruth said, studying my face. "Are you really going to be okay?"

"So many things are mixed up together, Ruth. I don't want to leave, and I ... "

"For what it's worth, I think you're doing the right thing," Ruth said. "Really. I know Andrew's sad to see you go, and of course Frankie and I would rather you stayed longer, but we understand. All of us."

Coming to Owl Creek had been such a relief, after so much trouble at home, so much not fitting, and I didn't want to have to leave again so soon. I was only just beginning to figure things out.

"What if I don't do the right things?" I asked. "What if I don't know what to say to Charlotte? Her twin sister is dying and they're six years old. What can I possibly say?"

Ruth locked eyes with me, her expression serious. "Sadie, you seem to always know the right thing to say. Truly. Maybe you don't know ahead of time, but when the moment comes, you just do. They say God gives people special gifts, and maybe that's one of yours."

Her words reminded me of Grant, and how I hadn't known what to say when the moment had come with the girls, or with Pips. "But I can't always . . ."

"They say God gives people special gifts, and I think that's one of yours," Ruth said, firmly.

"I've been messing that up a lot lately, Ruth. I didn't say anything at all to Karl, had no idea what to say to Pips, couldn't figure out how to stop the girls before they cheated in the design competition . . ."

"So since you made some mistakes, you're going to give up?" Ruth asked.

I closed my eyes, but all I could see was Charlotte's face. "No. I can't give up."

Ruth's mom knocked softly and opened the door. "Ruth, we should let Sadie get some sleep. Her flight is early tomorrow."

Ruth hugged me tight. "Good night, Sades. See you in the morning."

When the door closed behind them, I slipped under the covers and closed my eyes. But after fifteen minutes, I knew it was no use. I turned on the bedside light and took out my sketchbook.

The pages with the doorway in the creek, and the pages with the girl on the island seemed like they must go together somehow. Maybe after traveling through the watery doorway, the girl found herself on the island, isolated and alone. I started sketching, not thinking so much as just following the lines as they showed up on the paper. The girl was still on the island, but in the water, a hand reached up, a person in need. In the next frame, the girl stood, watching, wondering if she could swim that far. What if she swam out, only to drown too? Still, she couldn't stand by and not do anything at all. So, in the next frame, the girl dove into the water, and when she did, she found that like the creek, the water was a doorway to something else, a totally new place. Under the water's surface, just a little way down, were caverns and streams. The thrashing girl didn't have to drown, instead, she just needed to swim deeper.

Trust me.

If the ocean wasn't really the ocean, and I wasn't actually isolated on a tiny island, with no way to communicate with God, how was I supposed to know what was real? If I couldn't count on what I saw to be true?

Trust me.

And how was I supposed to know that everything would turn out okay? What if it didn't?

Trust me.

As the questions in my head settled, and my arguments

died out, I realized I wouldn't, couldn't know. Still, God had been with me this whole way, and now he was asking me to trust him. And no matter how hard that was, no matter how hard it would be for the girl to dive off the island into the ocean, I wouldn't know if there was more than I could see unless I did what God had asked. Unless I trusted.

I turned off the light, lay back, and whispered into the dark. *I'm still afraid.*

A few words from a prayer from the Book of Common Prayer slipped into my mind. I'd prayed these words every night for a while, earlier this year. The prayer was like a miniature gift, a kind of answer.

In thy mercy, grant us safe lodging, a holy rest, and peace at last. Amen.

Peace at last. A holy rest. I played the words over and over in my mind until I drifted off to sleep.

The morning was a whirlwind of breakfast and hugs and loading up the car. I slept for most of the flight and only started to get nervous again as the plane touched down in San Francisco.

Dad was waiting for me at the gate, and he wrapped me in his arms.

"Thank you for letting me come home, Dad."

"We missed you, Sades." He sounded so tired—the trial must not be going well.

I decided to get my idea out of the way right now. Dad would hate it, but maybe, just maybe, it would work. "Dad, I want to talk to Karl."

Dad stared at me. "Absolutely not, Sadie. No."

"You'd be there, Grant would be there, anyone else could be there, too. I just think … For some reason, I think he might listen to me."

"Sadie, I know you want to help Charlotte, and honestly, by coming home to spend time with her, that's helping. That's enough. There's no reason for you to talk to a crazy person."

"Karl told me all about his sister. He confided in me, Dad. I think he might listen to me, if I could only be brave enough to talk to him. I feel like I have to try."

"Let's walk." Dad took my bag and put his arm around me. "There are a lot of things you feel like you just have to do these days, aren't there, Sades? Give me a chance to think it over, okay? I'm not sure about the best thing to do."

Grant was waiting for us outside the security gate.

"Can I see Charlotte?" I asked, looking from one of them to the other.

"Tomorrow. She'll be at camp," Dad said. "Tonight, she's with her mom doing girls' night while her dad sits with Cici."

I needed to talk to Pips, then, so that we'd be ready for tomorrow. I couldn't go into camp with the strangeness still between us.

"Can Pips come over for dinner?" When Dad looked doubtful, I added, "I promise I won't ask for lots of hang out time. I know you need to work on the case. We just need to plan what to do for art tomorrow, and I want to be ready, for Charlotte. Okay, Dad?"

Dad studied my face, as though he was gauging how important my request was, in the scheme of everything.

Finally, he nodded. "Okay, Sadie. Grant and I both drove, so I can go back to work, and the two of you can go pick up Pippa. Call Mom and see if she's up for dinner at home, and if she's not, then you can go out to dinner wherever. Sound okay?"

"Yes, perfect. Thank you, Dad."

We idled outside Pippa's house about an hour later. Mom had been napping, so Grant and I had called Pips to invite her out to the Spaghetti Factory. She'd hesitated, and I knew she didn't want to see me very much, and probably especially not if we had to have our conversation in front of Grant. But since we didn't have any other options, and since I'd just flown all the way home from Owl Creek to be here for Charlotte, I wasn't in the backing down mood. We'd work this out, one way or another.

I knocked on the door, and Pips answered.

"Ready for some pasta?" I asked.

"You don't have to do that," Pips said.

"What?"

"Be all fake happy," Pips said. "At least be honest, okay?"

It was like a punch to my stomach. I'd already made things worse. So much for knowing the right thing to say when I needed to say it.

I swallowed hard and nodded. "Okay."

We went out to the Hummer, and I felt like we were walking to some terrible doom, like our friendship was about to be proclaimed officially dead. As soon as I thought the word, I thought of Cici and Charlotte. No. Neither Pips nor I was dying, not really. We weren't actually losing each other, and since we weren't, we had to give it our best shot, to try to work things out.

Even Grant noticed the quiet and turned up the radio. Fortunately, Spaghetti Factory was close to Pippa's house.

After Grant parked and turned off the engine, I asked. "Can Pips and I stay in the car for a minute?"

"I'll be right outside," Grant said, not asking questions.

I unclicked my seatbelt and went to sit in the seat next to Pippa. Since I didn't want to say the wrong thing, yet again, I picked at my fingernails, thinking.

"I don't know what to say, Sadie," Pippa said, finally breaking the silence.

"Sorry, Pips." I picked at my fingernails. "I didn't mean to make you talk first. I just can't figure out how to ..."

Pips nodded and for the first time in a long time, I thought we finally understood one another. At least about this.

"While I was away last year, I missed you so much, Pips," I said.

"I know, I missed you too," she said.

"And I guess I thought that when I came home, things would be the same. I didn't think about how much I had changed, and how much you would have changed."

"I don't think—" Pips began.

"You're my best friend, Pips," I said, quickly. "That hasn't changed."

"But . . ." Pippa said, hearing what I wasn't saying too.

"We can't expect everything to go back to the way it was before," I said. "I kept trying to find my old space, the space I used to fit into. But I'm different now, and so are you."

"I don't want things to change," Pippa said. "I want things to be okay with the girls, and with you too."

"For one thing, Pips, you have to stop protecting me. I need to tell the girls what I think about the secret club. I can't expect you to do that for me."

"But I didn't like how it was with Margo either," Pips said.

"I know, and you'll eventually figure out what you want to do about all of that. But like you said, I need to give you more room. To be you. And then I'll have room to be me, too. I don't want you to have to constantly feel like you're choosing sides."

Pips choked back a laugh. "I feel like we're breaking up."

I laughed then too. "It's not you, it's me."

Pippa snorted, and then gave me a serious look. "But you're my best friend, Sadie. You've always been my best friend."

I thought of the sketchbook she had sent me, when I'd first moved to Owl Creek. "Because we'll always be there for each other, when things are really, really good." I said and grinned. "Reason number one."

I played with my earring, trying to figure out how to say what I meant to say. "But being there for each other doesn't mean always agreeing on everything."

"No." Pips grinned back. "I guess not. Like, we'll never agree on whether hot fudge sundaes should be chocolate ice cream or vanilla."

"Right. Because they should be chocolate."

"Vanilla."

"Chocolate."

"Vanilla."

"I'll never give in, Pips."

"Promise?" she asked, and we both knew we weren't talking about ice cream anymore.

"Pinky-swear." I said, and we hooked pinkies.

"Then, let's see how fast Grant can run," she said.

We threw open the doors and raced Grant to the front of the restaurant.

Chapter 24

Even When You Don't Know

The minute I walked into camp, Charlotte tackled me, throwing herself into my arms. "You're back!"

I crouched down to look her in the eyes. So blue. I'd stayed up late last night, painting the drawing I'd made on the plane, of her jumping. I'd had to mix and mix to blend the perfect blue for her eyes. Later, when the time was right, I'd give her the painting.

"I missed you, Charlotte."

"I know what we should draw today," Charlotte said, her expression serious.

Since the kids had finished their picture books, some had gone on to do another, but Pips had been bringing drawing prompts each day, too, just in case. Last night, we'd decided to ask the kids to draw their favorite place. But I had no problem throwing out our lesson plan if Charlotte had an idea.

"What should we draw, Charlotte?"

"God," she said, simply.

Okay. I hadn't bargained for this. I glanced over my shoulder at Jess, and we exchanged a silent conversation that went something like:

Me: Is this a good idea?

Her: I think so.

Me: Okay…?

"God?" I asked Charlotte.

"How should we explain the assignment, Charlotte?" Jess asked.

"I know people don't know exactly what God looks like, but we can all just draw what we think, right?" Charlotte asked.

"Absolutely," Jess said, and then she called "Beetle!"

The kids turned, made their faces and shouted, "FACE!"

"Gather round, friends," Jess said. "We have a special assignment today."

Pips crossed the room to join us. "We're not drawing favorite places?"

"Would you like to explain this one, or should I?" Jess asked me.

"You," I said, more than grateful that Jess could read the uncertainty in my face.

"Charlotte had a great idea, friends," Jess said. "She was

thinking about what God looks like, and suggested that we all draw him the way we picture him in our minds. Of course, no one knows for sure what God looks like, so there's no right or wrong answer."

How had she explained that so easily? The kids had already begun to whisper to one another about their ideas, so she sent them off to tables to work.

Charlotte stared at her blank paper long after the other kids had started drawing. I went over to her.

"Are you all right, Charlotte?"

She squeezed her eyes shut for a few seconds but when she opened them, she shook her head. "I can't see anything, Sadie."

"What do you mean?"

"Usually, you ask us a question, and I whisper it in my mind to Cici, and she sends me pictures, ones I can see in my head. And I know what to draw. But today she's not sending me anything. It's just . . . blank."

I knew Charlotte believed, absolutely, that she and her sister could talk across miles this way, and who was I to say she couldn't? It sounded impossible to me, but I'd never been a twin. And I knew that feeling close to Cici like this, whether or not it was real, was one of the only things keeping Charlotte afloat. Probably she had asked to draw God for this very reason, to try to understand what Cici was feeling or thinking about sickness, about life and death.

"I asked her what God looks like, and she isn't answering. Why isn't she, Sadie?"

I couldn't lie to her, and even though I wanted to smooth it over, she was too smart to not see through empty, soothing words.

So finally I said, "I don't know, Charlotte."

Her eyes filled with tears, and I was sure I'd said the wrong thing. But then, she blinked at me and said, "I don't think she knows. She wants me to tell her what God looks like and I am afraid I'll be wrong. I've never seen him."

The words could have come out of my own mouth, about what to say to the girls, about what to say to Charlotte, right now. "I'm afraid I'll be wrong a lot of the time, too, Charlotte."

"But you tell us what you think," Charlotte said, leaping to my defense. "You're brave, and you tell us when you're not sure, too. When you tell me what you think, it helps me see what I think better too."

This girl. I'd barely known her for two weeks, and she'd completely stolen my heart. "You know, I never thought of it like that, Charlotte."

"Maybe I should just draw what I think God looks like, then," Charlotte said. "For Cici. And maybe my picture will help her see her own. Do you think that might happen, Sadie?"

I wrapped my arms around Charlotte and squeezed her tight. "Charlotte, yes. I think so."

I let her go, and she picked up a purple pencil and started to sketch. I circled the room, looking at the pictures. Many showed some variation of God looking like a grandfather in a big chair surrounded by clouds. Other drawings were predictable, because I knew these kids. Fritz, for instance, had drawn a huge superhero that took up most of the page. But he hadn't drawn the face. He'd drawn his caped hero from shoulders down.

"Why didn't you draw the head, Fritz?" I asked.

"Because God looks different to every person," Fritz said. "His face, I mean. And in the Bible stories people don't see his whole face, anyway. Just parts. Like the corner of his nose."

Pips joined me at Fritz's desk.

"But he's the one superhero that has every power. No limit. Well, except the limits he puts on himself, because he wants us to do stuff for ourselves sometimes too."

By now, Jess had joined us too. "Fritz, I think you're on for the sermon next Sunday. How do you feel about preaching to our congregation?"

Fritz's eyes went wide and Jess started to laugh. "I'm only kidding. But I'd love to use your drawing, if you'll let me. What do you think?"

Fritz nodded, and went on to explain all the other details to Jess as Pips and I walked away to check on the other students. I wandered back toward Charlotte, who had folded her drawing up into a small square.

"Do you want to show me your drawing, Charlotte?" I asked.

She nodded solemnly. "Someday, Sadie. But today, my drawing is just for Cici. Because she needs it most of all."

I smiled and put my hand on her shoulder. "Yep, Charlotte. I think you're absolutely right."

All through camp, I braced myself for the phone call from the hospital, but it didn't come. Maybe Cici would pull through after all. Pippa did get a phone call, though, from the girls. When all the kids had left to go to other activities, she sat and fidgeted.

"What is it, Pips?" I asked.

"Alice wants us to come over to Bri's house."

"Why?"

"Margo had a change of heart, and the girls want to work out what to do."

"Time for me to say what I really think, huh?" I sighed. "Better sooner than later."

"You don't have to," Pips said protectively. "I mean, not today. You already have so much …"

I raised an eyebrow at her. "You're protecting me again."

"Yeah, okay," Pips said. "Well, if you want to."

Grant pulled up at almost the same time as Alice's mom, and we caravanned over to Bri's house. On the drive over, Dad called and asked to talk to me.

"You're sure you want to talk to Karl, Sadie?" Dad asked. "I'm just not sure …"

"I know you don't want to involve me, Dad," I said. "But I'm involved already. And I need a chance to speak my mind."

I could almost see Dad shaking his head on the other end of the phone. "That's what Grant said too. That it wouldn't be resolved for you until you'd stood up to Karl yourself."

The words slammed into me, and finally I understood what I needed to say to the girls.

"Tell Grant that Karl will be coming to the house at two o'clock, and that I'd like him to stay for the conversation."

I hung up with Dad and told Grant what was going on. It was already one o'clock, so I could only stay at Bri's for about a half hour. I promised Grant I'd be quick, and then Pips and I went inside and up to Bri's room.

The girls had gathered Bri's beanbags and were sitting in a tight circle, as though they were afraid someone might overhear them.

Bri was explaining, "She's going to tell the judges that we trapped her into cheating."

"She's such a liar!" Juliet said. "She would have cheated anyway."

Only then did the girls notice that Pips and I had come into the room, and they all clammed up.

"Look," I said. "I hate this whole secret club thing, and I should have said so a long time ago."

Alice threw me an irritated look. "So, what is that, like a too-late I told you so?"

"No. When Pips told me about the video, I thought it sounded like blackmail, and I should have said something to all of you. But I didn't."

"The video stopped Jaylia," Juliet protested.

"Right. And that's what I've been trying to figure out this whole time," I said. "Like Pips said, you've been helping.

It's not like you should lie down and let the bullies walk all over you."

"So what do you suggest?" Alice asked, her voice dripping with sarcasm.

"Honestly, I don't know," I said. "I think we have to figure out how to stand up to people without bullying them."

"The teachers won't help us," Bri said. "We tried that."

"I know," I said. "But look what happened when Margo came into the store last week. What would have happened if we'd stood up to her right then? That would have been better than sneaking around and cheating, right?"

"Okay, so maybe we cheated. But it worked at first," Bri said defensively.

"And now it's all a mess," Pips said.

Grant honked, and I knew I'd taken too long.

"When are you talking to the judges?" I asked.

"Monday," Bri said.

"Okay, then," I said. "I'll be there too."

"You didn't cheat," Alice snapped. "You weren't even part of it."

"No," I said. "But we should stick together on this."

When I left, they all looked miserable, and I felt pretty miserable too. But I knew getting everything out in the open would feel better than bottling it up. Like when I'd finally told Dad the truth about Karl.

I didn't feel much like talking on the way home. Now that I was about to face Karl, I wasn't sure I'd say the right thing, or even be able to speak at all. But I had to do this for

Charlotte. And actually, for me, too. Karl had backed me into too many corners and terrified me and I'd never had the chance to tell him what I really thought. And here was my chance.

Please help me. Give me the right words to say.

Chapter 25

Hold My Hand

"Here's what I want to say," I said, once I had situated myself on the couch next to Dad, across from crazy Karl, whose face was already red with anger. Dad had promised we'd listen to Karl only after I'd had a chance to speak.

My stomach twisted with fear, but I took a deep breath and began. "I've been thinking about your sister," I said, cautiously. "About what you told me in the elevator. I think you're wrong."

Karl made an angry noise and Dad shot him a warning look.

"I don't know how long it has been since your sister died," I pressed on. "But look how much you still love her, how much you've done for her."

"Right, which is why—" Karl began, and Dad held up his hand.

I stared down at my hands for a minute, trying to put what I wanted to say into words. "The past few weeks, I've been working with Charlotte, at camp. And I ... love her. Even though she's so sad—not being able to see Cici, knowing Cici might die—but still, Charlotte is like this little ... light. She lights up the room when she walks in. Tyler knew his kids might get sick, and he had them anyway. All he wants to do is find a way to help them stay healthy. To help Charlotte stay healthy. She deserves that chance, doesn't she? What if it had been your sister, before she got sick? Wouldn't she deserve a chance?"

Karl stood, pushing his chair back a few feet. "I'm done with this conversation."

"I'd be angry too," I said as he started out of the room. "If I lost Charlotte. But deep down, I'd have to admit I loved her. And that loving her was worth it. You can't just block out everything and everyone that might hurt you."

Karl stared at me for a moment, and then said, "She looked like you, a little. My sister." And then he was gone.

Mom came in with the phone in her hand, her face pale. "Matthew? Sadie?"

"Cici?" Dad asked.

"They're letting Charlotte see her."

I didn't understand. Wasn't it a good thing if Charlotte could finally see her sister? "Why do you look so upset?"

"They don't feel it's essential to protect Cici from infection anymore," Mom said.

And then I understood. "Because they think she's dying?"

"Charlotte's mom called and asked if we'd come."

I couldn't speak over the sudden lump in my throat. On our way out, I realized maybe this was the time to give Charlotte her painting. I hurried up to get it, scratched Higgins ears as I closed him in the house, and ran for the Hummer, where Mom, Dad, and Grant already waited. When we arrived at the hospital, Charlotte stood, small, pale-faced, in the hallway, holding her mom's hand.

"I waited for you, Sadie," she said. "I want you to come with me."

Even though her eyes were dry, understanding sparked deep, too. Someone had explained to her that Cici wouldn't be with us much longer.

Charlotte slipped her hand out of her mom's and into mine. "I want you to tell Cici about seeing what's invisible. If ... when ... I can't see her anymore, I want her to know I'll always be looking for her."

I swallowed hard. If Charlotte wasn't going to cry, then I wasn't either. "Okay. We'll tell her."

"The doctors think we should limit Charlotte's visit to five minutes. Just in case ..." Charlotte's mom's voice broke and she turned away.

Just in case. So they were holding on to the tiny hope that maybe Cici could pull out of this. But they also knew that Charlotte had to say goodbye to her sister, because this might be her last chance.

I squeezed Charlotte's hand. "Are you ready?"

She nodded.

We pushed through the door into the darkened room. Cici lay under the covers, hardly taking up any of the adult-sized bed. Tyler sat next to her, holding her hand.

"You're here," he whispered, and I wasn't sure whether he was talking to Charlotte or me.

He stood, and when he set down Cici's hand, I could barely distinguish between the white of her skin and the white of the sheet. He gave Charlotte his chair. She gripped my fingers even as she sat down, so I just stood beside her. Charlotte never took her eyes off Cici.

Cici's head was bald from the chemo, and her eyebrows and lashes were gone too.

When Charlotte leaned in and whispered, "Cici?" she didn't open her eyes.

"She can't ..." Tyler began, but Charlotte just went on.

"It's okay if you can't open your eyes right now, Cici," she said. "I brought my friend to see you. Sadie. She's been helping me draw, the one I told you about who paints the wind. Tell her, Sadie."

How could I resist Charlotte when she looked at me like that? I cleared my throat. "Sometimes when I close my eyes, outside in the wind, the air feels thick and strong ..."

"Like God is wrapping round her in a giant hug," Charlotte continued for me. "And that's what I wanted to tell you, Cici, that you don't have to know what God looks like because all you have to do is close your eyes and you can feel him."

Charlotte let go of my hand to take a folded piece of paper out of her pocket. Her drawing.

"Cici, I drew this for you. I don't know what God looks like, but this is what I imagine. You'll have to tell me if I'm right ..." she paused and breathed deep. "... If you have to go. But if you can stay ..." Charlotte's voice broke off.

I wanted to hug her, tell her everything would be all right. But of course, I didn't know what would happen. Chances were, things would become very, very difficult.

Charlotte took Cici's finger and helped her trace the lines of the drawing.

"Since you can't see it with your eyes," she said.

Maybe because they were twins, and maybe because they knew each other so well, Charlotte was able to understand what any other six-year-old couldn't. Somehow, here with Cici, Charlotte seemed much more whole than she'd ever been at camp. Which should be impossible. Most kids would be terrified, I'd guess, or something, but Charlotte seemed strangely at home.

Charlotte refolded the paper and pressed it into Cici's hand. As she did, Cici's eyes fluttered, once, twice, and then she opened them and locked eyes with her sister. No one breathed. Finally, Cici breathed out, and her eyes drifted closed.

"Daddy, Cici needs the doctor," Charlotte said, turning those blue eyes on him.

Tyler rushed out of the room, and came back with a doctor. He checked the monitors and Cici's pulse and gave a quick nod. "We need to take her back up to quarantine. Somehow ... I can't say how, but ..."

"She's getting better, isn't she?" Charlotte asked him.

The doctor gave Charlotte a quick once-over, head to toe, as though he was judging whether to answer her question at all. Finally, he said, "Her fever broke, and her vitals ... yes. Something happened—I don't understand what."

Then, the room filled with a flurry of masked and gloved nurses, who whisked Charlotte and me out of the room, and seconds later, hurried Cici up the hall on a rolling gurney.

"What happened?" Charlotte's mom was on her feet. "Where are they taking her, Tyler?"

His face was hard to read. He took Charlotte's mom into his arms.

"They're taking her back to quarantine," he said into her hair.

"But that means ..." she said.

"Yes," was all Tyler said.

Chapter 26

Catch the Wind

After they rolled Cici out of the room, Charlotte finally started to sob, huge, racking sobs like half of herself had been ripped away. I wrapped my arms around her and rubbed her back, and looked helplessly at Mom. We couldn't just sit here in the hospital and wait. Charlotte's parents asked if we could watch her, and so in a few minutes, we found ourselves back out in the Hummer, with no definite plan.

"Seems like we should go somewhere," Mom said. "Not just home."

Charlotte had finally cried herself out and now she was pale, and didn't look like she was in any condition to make decisions. Her painting was in the back, and I wanted to give that to her, but not in the car.

What now? I silently asked, and then smiled in spite of

219

myself. Maybe I wasn't the girl on the island with the messages in the bottles anymore. Maybe, finally, I had dove into the water. And suddenly, I had my answer.

"Can we go to the beach?" I asked Mom.

"It is a windy day," Mom answered, as though she'd read my mind.

Charlotte leaned her head against my arm and fell asleep on the drive over the mountains. When the car stopped, she opened her eyes and stretched.

"Where are we?"

I smiled. "I'm going to teach you how to catch the wind."

"We'll wait for you here," Mom said, and even though sadness panged through me, thinking of catching the wind without her, I knew this was right too. Charlotte and I, catching the wind together.

"What does that mean ... Catch the wind?" Charlotte asked.

"You'll see. But first, I have a surprise."

I helped her down from the back seat and took her around to the back of the Hummer. When I threw the doors open, she gasped.

"It's me, jumping!" She threw her arms around me and squeezed. "Can I have it?"

"It's yours," I took her hand and we ran out across the sand.

I pointed at the bluff.

"We're going up there?" she asked.

"I'll help you," I said.

We scaled the rocks, and when we reached the top, I helped Charlotte find solid footholds. I reached out my hands, face toward the ocean. She threw her hands wide too, and air rushed through our outstretched fingers. As we stood, with the wind swirling around us, pink tipped the clouds, the beginning of sunset.

"I'm going to catch some extra and put it in my pocket to take back to Cici. Do you think she'll like that?" Charlotte asked.

"She'll love that," I said, feeling warmth seep into my skin, not from the wind, but from what vibrated through the wind, the feeling of God, close, as close as my next breath.

"I feel purple and green and red," Charlotte shouted over the wind. "What do you feel?"

"Electric blue and teal," I answered.

"And sparkly gold." Charlotte spun all the way around before finding her footholds again.

"How could I forget the sparkly gold?" I asked.

Our laughter wove together, spinning out into the salty air.

THE END

From Sadie's Sketchbook

Shades of Truth

Naomi Kinsman

★ *Publishers Weekly* starred review

It's Going to Be a Bear of a Year

Sadie thought she'd have a perfect fresh start when she moved to Owl Creek, Michigan, but finding her place in her new school proves harder than expected. In this divided town, her father's job mediating between bear hunters and researchers doesn't help her social life. Sadie's art instructor encourages her to express herself through her sketchbook and develop her newfound talent. As everything swirls around her, Sadie must learn what it means to have faith when you don't have all the answers.

We want to hear from you. Please send your comments about this book to us in care of zreview@zondervan.com. Thank you.